Brilliant Disguise

Brilliant Disguise

Mark Berman

Writer's Showcase
San Jose New York Lincoln Shanghai

Brilliant Disguise

Writer's Showcase
an imprint of iUniverse.com, Inc.

For information address:
iUniverse.com, Inc.
5220 S 16th, Ste. 200
Lincoln, NE 68512
www.iuniverse.com

ISBN: 0-595-18669-6

Printed in the United States of America

Now my bed is cold
Lost in the darkness of our love
God have mercy on the man
Who doubts what he's sure of.
Bruce Springsteen, "Brilliant Disguise"

PART I

-I-

As it does unfailingly at 6:00 every morning, the alarmclock goes off. As he does unfailingly at 6:00:05, Bill Press grunts. He rolls over. He's got that horrible tasting breath that you get in the morning. It's particularly sour this morning. When you're a kid, they tell you the sandman puts the crust in your eyes. Does that mean there is a badbreath man, too, with a bucket full of some sort of foul smelling solution?

Bill begrudgingly drags himself out of bed at 6:19, after the 6:15 news break, which begins with the presumably smiling newswoman saying that exactly at 7:22 this morning, summer officially begins. The next story is about the impending race for the U.S. Senate. What gives her the right to run for the Senate from our state? She's never even lived here. She wants to take the job away from a deserving man, who's spent his whole life serving us. She's only riding the coattails of her husband, anyway. Without him, who would she be?

Bill looks at himself in the mirror. Looks pretty good. No grey hairs, no receding hairline, still trim and lean. These are the years, the early 30's, when guys start going to hell. They start losing their hair, their hair that is speckled with grey. They get that pouch. But not Bill. He's looking pretty darn good. His breath is another story. He picks up the nearly empty tube of toothpaste. He squeezes as hard as he can, until his brush is filled with the sweet tasting gel that will start the day out right.

Helen knocks on the door. She wants the bathroom. Bill is still in the shower. The door is locked. Helen insists on walking into the bathroom when he's in there. Locking the door is something he could never do when he was living with his parents. Bill's mom would not let him lock the bathroom door, just in case he became unconscious, or overcome by bathroom fumes, or fell into the toilet. If the door is locked, how could she come in and save him? So now in his own home, he's taken to locking the door. He finishes up his shower real quick, dries his hair, puts in his contacts, and relinquishes the room to Helen. Did I wash my body?, Bill thinks. He knows he washed his hair. But Helen was rushing him so, he can't remember soaping up. He tries to smell himself. But he can't tell. He'd like to take another shower just to be on the safe side, but there's no time. Once again, Helen has disrupted his morning.

Bill goes to his closet, to pick the clothing of the day. Bill has become a real fashionplate at work. For today, Bill picks his blue rayon shirt that everyone thinks is silk, his light blue Calvin Kleins, and one of his wild ties. This one has purplish flowers on it, like leaves on a tree. This woman Sarah at work calls it his 'Jungle Tie.'

Bill is out of tokens for the tunnel. So he goes to the little miniature safe where he puts his change, and counts out 14 quarters for the toll. This way, he can go to the toll machine, and save time. Bill hates it when people go into the exact change line, and then don't have the change or the token. So they've got to back out, and delay the whole process. Either you have the change or you don't. Don't go in on a hunch. Bill puts the 14 quarters in his pocket.

Bill goes back into the bedroom. It's a large room. There's space between the bed and Helen's dresser to easily walk through. In their first apartment, that space was barely a foot. Negotiating through the space without hitting his leg on the dresser or the bed was rare indeed. Bill usually bypassed it all together, and walked over the bed to get to his side. Helen never had any business on his side, so she never had to worry about the tight space. Helen is toweling off. She looks at herself in the mirror and sighs. Women are never happy with the way they look. Helen is no different. She thought she was a little flabby, so she dropped 20 pounds. But now, she complains her breasts are too small. Seems that's where most of the weight came from. That was the one advantage when Helen put on some weight. Her breasts got bigger. But it really didn't make up for the roll she got in her belly. So Bill likes the new, improved firmer Helen. But bigger breasts would be nice just the same.

Bill picks up his wallet, keys, and Ray-Bans, and kisses Helen on the cheek. Helen tells him to make sure he comes home on time. Her mother's coming over for dinner. Bill grunts for the second time this morning, and heads downstairs. While on the way down, he recounts his quarters, just to make sure he took 14. He doesn't want to be like the idiots who have to back out of the exact change lane because they didn't take enough quarters from their safe.

Summertime. It's a time of year Bill has always held dear. Yet it's a time of year he fears. A certain freedom prevails in this season, probably going back to his school days. People act differently in the summer. That's the time things happen, albeit usually temporary, summertime things. But sometimes things last. That's when he fell in love with Helen. That's when he proposed to Helen. That's when they got married. Bill hates change. And if things are ever going to change, it'll be in the summer. Bill thinks if he can just get through the summer, he'll be all right. Yet Bill experiences a depression of sorts when Labor Day arrives. More often than not, nothing happens to him, and he regrets wasting the best time of the year.

Bill gets to his car, and spreads the 14 quarters out on the passenger seat. As they drop from his hand, he counts them again. One could have gotten caught in the sewing in his pocket. Three dollars and fifty cents to go from one borough to another. What a scam. The people who run this city are doing all they can to drain money from its people. Bill can remember his father tossing two quarters into the basket, and the gate going up. Now it's 14. Bill takes the opportunity to count his quarters again. Maybe one fell behind the seat.

Helen's mother. The Disagreeable Widow, that's what Bill has taken to calling her. Behind her back, of course. What's she coming over for? So she can criticize everything Bill and Helen do? The way their furniture is arranged.

Helen's cooking. Even the way the vines from the plants are hanging from the bookshelf. And then she and Helen start speaking Italian, her mother's native tongue, making Bill feel left out. They're probably talking about him. With him in the room. That's worse than whispering.

Driving is a great time to think. Bill thinks back to Helen's naked body. When Bill first met Helen, he thought she was the most beautiful girl in the world. He'd look at other girls, and no one would be more beautiful. Love will do that to you. But now, after being together nine years, six of those years married, everyone seems to look better. Bill looks at girls, and it's always Why can't Helen have her eyes? She's got bigger tits than Helen. She's got a better body. Bill wonders why that is. Helen is still as beautiful as she ever was. Guys still look at her. Bill hates that. All of his friends comment on how great she looks. Bill likes that. So why all of a sudden does every other girl look more enticing?

Bill approaches the toll booth. With one hand on the wheel and one eye on the road, Bill's other hand and eye count his quarters. Still 14. As he lets them go into the little basket, he counts them again…ten, eleven, twelve, thirteen, fourteen. Bill glances at the clock on his radio. It reads 7:22. The gate goes up. Bill passes through.

-2-

"Hello, Mrs. Harrington? This is Bill Press. I'm calling you today from the 'Daily News.' How are you on this first day of summer?"

"Fine," the already on-her-guard Mrs. Harrington answers.

"That's good." Bill works for a telephone marketing company called 'Prevail Marketing.' The company is hired to sell everything from credit cards to vacuum cleaners to magazine subscriptions over the phone. Today, Bill is selling the 'Daily News.'

Mrs. Harrington decides to cut this conversation short. "Listen, I'm not really interested in a subscription."

"And I'm not interested in selling you a subscription to the 'Daily News.'" The sale has begun.

"You're not?" Mrs. Harrington's interest is peaked.

"Well, sure, my job is to sell subscriptions to this fine newspaper. But what I'm mostly concerned about is you, Mrs. Harrington."

"Really?" Mrs. Harrington is both flattered and suspicious.

"Yes. You seem like the type of woman who stays informed on the issues facing our city and our country today."

"Yes I am. I watch the news on television every day."

"That's what I was afraid of."

"Why?"

"Well, uh, nothing. I don't want to waste your time. Have a nice summer, Mrs. Harrington." Bill waits to hang up. And right on cue, Mrs. Harrington says "Wait, what's wrong with getting the news from T.V.?"

"It's just that regardless of how much news there is on a particular day, or how important a news story is, everything must get crammed into the same amount of space. In a newspaper, specifically the 'Daily News,' the paper can expand if there's more news. A major story can get several pages, while on T.V., it's got to fit into 20 seconds."

"Hmm, I never thought of that."

"And do you want your news interpreted by some charm school news anchor, or would you like to read it and interpret it on your own?"

"Well, on my own, of course."

"And where do you think T.V. gets its stories from?"

"The newspapers?"

"Of course. And they get most of their stories from the 'Daily News.' So can I put you down for a year?"

Like a cinderblock falling on her head, Mrs. Harrington realizes she's being sold. "So you are trying to sell me a subscription. You're just a salesman."

"Mrs. Harrington, I'm insulted. My job is to make sure you are informed as best as you can. And you cheapen it by calling me a salesman."

"I'm sorry."

"So why don't you try it just for the summer? If you don't like it, you just call me back the day after Labor Day, and not only will I cancel your subscription, you'll get all of your money back."

"Well..."

"And this refund is not coming from the 'Daily News.' It'll come right from my own pocket. That's how much I care about you."

Partly to get off the phone, and partly out of guilt, Mrs. Harrington agrees. Bill ends the conversation with "and don't forget, the day after Labor Day, you just call me if you're not satisfied. Just ask for Bill Press." Bill has pulled this "refund-out-of-my-own-pocket" ploy many times in the past, and it seems to be effective. It seems to make people feel too guilty to call back if they think some poor slob who makes a living selling things over the telephone will have to shell out the money.

It's tactics like these that have made Bill Press the best tele-marketer at Prevail Marketing. It's his ability to sense a customer's weak point, clamp down hard on it, and not let go until Bill gets what he wants.

"Nice tie." It's Sarah, the one who likes Bill's ties. As she says this, she lifts the tie up off Bill's chest, and lets it gently drop. "You want to go to lunch today?"

"Sure." Bill and Sarah go to lunch every day. Yet she feels the need to ask him this, as if this unspoken bond between the two does not exist. "Where do you want to go?"

"I can go for a thick bloody burger."

"I really shouldn't. The doctor says my cholesterol's too high. How about pizza?"

"No. I really want a big red slab of meat."

Although she's making it seem so appetizing, Bill still refuses. He comes up with Chinese as a compromise. She can get a beef dish, he can get chicken. But the idea is struck down. Then Sarah says, "Maybe we just won't go together

today." But as Sarah knows full well, Bill hates to eat alone. So he gives in. He'll be eating a big red slab of meat for lunch. Sarah is smiling.

Bill likes Sarah. Exactly why he's not sure. Her personality makeup is almost hateful to Bill. She's selfish, vain, manipulative, image-conscience, and unfriendly. She never reveals anything about herself. And just when Bill gets disgusted with her, she gives him a look. She'll face him three-quarters, and flash her blue eyes. It's the sexiest look he's ever seen. Maybe that's why he likes her. And maybe that's why he's got this unspoken bond with her. Or does he? Bill simply can't figure women out. Just when he thinks Sarah likes him as much as he likes her, she turns around and treats him as if he's just another co-worker, and not the guy she would be sleeping with if Bill wasn't married. Does she send out these mixed signals on purpose? Or is he just another co-worker? Bill has no answer.

Bill and Sarah walk out into the noon heat. The first day of summer, and it's already 80 degrees, with humidity to match. But Bill looks cool in his Ray-Ban sunglasses, and he knows it. But just to make sure, Bill looks into the windows of passing stores to see his reflection, to see if the desired effect is there. Looking into the windows, he sees that he and Sarah make a handsome looking couple. Bill at six feet towering over the five foot, four inch Sarah. And Sarah appears to be a good match for Bill. Bill looks into the window, and wonders if he should mention it to Sarah. But he thinks better of it, not knowing if she'd even care.

They reach the 'Burger Joint', and are seated. Bill carefully slips his Ray-Bans into its protective case, and places it on the table. Sarah looks into a mirror she has taken from her purse, to check if the hot June wind did any damage to her newly peroxided hair. "So, what are you and your wife doing for vacation?" Sarah knows Helen's name. He refers to her as 'Helen' in conversation. Yet Sarah always refers to her as 'your wife'.

"Nothing. We're saving our money to buy another house. What are you doing?"

"My parents have a house in The Hamptons. I'll probably go out there for a week. Hey, the week I'm there, why don't you come out for the weekend?"

Bill's face drops. Did she just invite him out for a weekend of love? She must have. She didn't mention 'your wife.' For the first time in the two years he has known her, Sarah actually may have let her feelings for him show. But Bill's happiness is reeled back in when he looks back down at his ringfinger. "I can't. What with being married and all." Without blinking, Sarah shoots back "I MEANT you AND your wife." "Oh, well, then, maybe," a clearly disappointed Bill stammers. Bill is hoping Sarah continues the conversation, by asking what he thought she meant by the invitation. But being Sarah, she doesn't ask. Instead, they both place orders for their big red slabs of meat.

If Sarah invited Bill and 'his wife,' then she must go out there with someone. But Sarah never mentions it. Bill can't imagine she'd go there alone. In fact, Bill can't imagine anyone doing anything alone. Bill looks around the restaurant, and sees several people lunching alone. There's nothing wrong with it really, just a worker going out for lunch. Bill would never eat alone. Everyone would be looking at him, he thinks. Bill never shops alone. Bill is never alone. The thought scares him to death.

The burgers arrive. And just like Sarah wanted, they are big, and red, and dripping. Bill picks up his burger, and takes a bite. He then puts it down, picks up his napkin, wipes his hands, puts down the napkin, and takes another bite of the burger. Then he eats a couple of french fries and takes a sip of his Pepsi, making sure to ration them out, so at the end, he'll have equal amounts of burger, fries, and Pepsi left, so as not to finish one too soon. The process of wiping his hands after touching each food group forces

Bill to continually turn his napkin inside-out, until his lunch is methodically eaten.

Sarah, on the other hand, has no eating plan. Bill watches in amazement as she gobbles down all of her French fries before finishing her burger, and finishes her Diet Coke so early, she must order another one. Poor planning. Maybe it's this lack of attention to details that makes Sarah one of the worst tele-marketers at Prevail Marketing. She doesn't pay enough attention to the intricate details of the people she's talking to, to convince them of anything. Or maybe she just doesn't care.

-3-

The drive home from work is anything but pleasant. Traffic is backed up, and the sultry early summer night combined with car fumes makes Bill hot. He loosens his tie, then finally rolls up the windows, and turns on the air conditioning. He'll assume the risk of stalling in the bumper-to-bumper traffic with the air on. With the air conditioner cooling him off, the trip is tolerable. Bill loves the feeling of the cold air blowing on his face, knowing outside is sweltering. He can just roll up the windows, and shut it all out.

But what he can't shut out is that when he gets home, the Disagreeable Widow will already be there. It's rare for her to be coming for dinner on a weekday. Usually, she comes on Sundays. Bill thinks she picks that day to ruin the football season for him. But then he figures she's probably not that smart.

Just like he predicted, there's Helen and her mother, sitting at the kitchen table, talking Italian. They stop when he comes in, as if he can understand what they're talking about. He kisses Helen, then says "hi" to her mother, and begrudgingly kisses her on the cheek. Bill doesn't even kiss his own mother every time he sees her, but he must kiss the Disagreeable Widow, Helen orders.

Bill sits down at the table. Helen gives Bill a talk-to-her look. Bill makes a face, and asks "So, how are you?"

But Bill gets no answer, because Helen's mother is not facing him, and she thinks he's talking to Helen. A simple solution to this would be to address her by name or title. But the only problem is, Bill doesn't call her anything. He can't call her by her first name. Helen won't allow it. He can't call her Mrs. Gulzilianio, because he can't pronounce it. So the only thing left is Mom. But the word won't roll off Bill's tongue. He has a mom. And she's not her. So Bill just waits for eye contact before talking to her. Finally, Helen says, "Ma, Bill's talking to you."

"Oh," She says. "I'ma fine."

"Good."

"And how area you?"

"All right." She then turns to Helen and says something in Italian. They must be talking about him. Why else would they have to speak a foreign language? Whatever she said, Helen pacifies her by saying "It'll be all right." She says this in English, leading Bill to believe things will not be all right.

While Bill goes upstairs to change, the two women go off to the stove, where the pasta is cooking. Helen tastes it. "It's not done yet." So her mother tastes it. "Yes it is."

"It's too hard."

"But that'sa the way itsa supposed to be."

"But Bill doesn't like it hard, you know that." But she doesn't listen. She just picks up the pot, and dumps it into the colander in the sink. Helen just shakes her head, and takes the roast beef out of the oven. While Helen goes for the electric knife, her mother is reaching for the big fork and knife to cut the roast beef. "Ma, I'll do it."

"No, I'll do it. I alwaysa cut the meat."

"But you cut it too thick. Bill likes it thin."

"Ah, Bill doesn't know how to eat." But she's puts down the knife and fork, leaving Helen to do the cutting.

Bill spends the maximum time he can upstairs. He even flosses his teeth to kill time. When he finally comes down, the pasta is already on the table. Bill puts his fork into it. He looks at Helen. "It's too hard." The Disagreeable Widow keeps her head down, eating her pasta. Bill makes a face, then tries to twirl his linguine on his fork. But he can't because they are short. "And who broke the pasta?" As if he has to ask. Bill likes his pasta long. And he's made it clear to Helen's mother time and time again that in her house, she can break the pasta all she wants. It's her house, and he'll play by her rules. But in his house, it's his rules, and she's got to abide by them. But he doesn't bother saying any of this. He just chokes down his hard, short pasta, the tension growing inside him with each unpleasant bite.

Bill dreads the next course. He's sure Helen's mother insisted on cutting the roast beef. But much to his surprise, it's thinly cut. Bill looks at Helen, and thanks her with his eyes. The evening will not be a total wreck.

They retire to the living room. Except for the pasta incident, the Disagreeable Widow hasn't been too disagreeable at all. Something must be up, thinks Bill. She's being too nice. And by 'too nice,' Bill means she hasn't been a bitch.

Before she comes into the living room, Helen's mother turns off the kitchen light. So Bill must get up, and turn the light on. Helen and Bill have a very small, two bedroom townhouse. The downstairs consists of just two rooms; the living room, and a galley-type kitchen. Off the kitchen is the dinette area, which is right next to the living room. So turn the kitchen light off, and the whole downstairs gets dark. Bill doesn't like to sit in a dark house. He likes it nice and bright, all the lights on. Helen's mother, however, sits in her dark house, with just a lamp on. Bill gets an eerie feeling sitting in a dark house.

"Why don'taya leavea the light off? You'rea wasting electricity."

"Because I like the lights on. In your house, you can turn the lights off."

Helen senses an argument, so she changes the subject. "Mom has good news."

"Oh yeah, what?"

"She sold her house."

"Really?" Bill is genuinely surprised. He didn't know it was for sale.

"She's all alone there. She doesn't need that big house." Helen sounds defensive.

"Hey, you don't have to defend her move. I agree. I'm glad she's out of there. The area is changing. In a couple of years, I'm afraid it'll be dangerous for a woman to walk around there." They're talking as if Helen's mother were not in the room. Bill addresses her. "So what are you going to do, buy a condo?"

Helen's mother looks at Helen. They look at Bill. "I'ma gonna livea here."

"Oh, you want to buy our place," Bill deduces. "That's perfect. We want to move to a bigger house anyway. Now, we won't have kill ourselves finding a buyer." Bill is happy for the first time since he walked in the door.

"No, you don't understand," says Helen. "Mom is going to live with us."

"Live with us?"

"Yeah. We have the extra room upstairs." The extra room, with Bill's computer and his weights and all of his stuff.

"Uh huh, uh huh, uh huh," is all Bill can muster.

"And she'll pay us rent. That will help us save money to buy another house."

"Uh huh, uh huh, uh huh."

"And she's all alone. No one should have to live alone. Especially if they have somewhere to go."

"Uh huh, uh huh, uh huh. When is this going to happen?"

"Over the weekend. She's got to be out by then, because she closes on Monday."

"Monday? Doesn't it take a couple of months for the buyer to get a mortgage and all that stuff."

"Well," Helen stammers, "she sold the house a couple of months ago."

"And you didn't tell me?"

"Uh huh, uh huh, uh huh."

Bill walks upstairs, and stops at the spare room. He looks in, and sees his weights and desk and computer and the little chest with his crap in it and his safe with his change on top of it. He walks into the bathroom. He hates the thought of sharing his bathroom with another person. Now, he'll have to wipe the toilet seat every time he wants to sit down. Just like in a public restroom or at a friend's house, on those rare occasions when Bill just can't wait until he gets home.

He walks into the bedroom, and easily glides through the space between the bed and the dresser. The June night is hot, so Bill reaches up, and pulls the chain on the ceiling fan. Helen is getting undressed, throwing her dirty clothes

in a pile on her side of the bed. Helen is looking around the bedroom, presumably trying to figure out how to move the spare room into the bedroom, to make room for the Disagreeable Widow.

Bill and Helen move about the room in silence as they prepare for bed. More and more of their time together has been spent in silence, Bill thinking about work or about Sarah, Helen thinking about whatever it is women think about. Bill is completely clueless about this. Bill loves women. He'll be the first one to tell you he'd rather be around women than men. But just what is going though their minds is a complete mystery. Why they do the things they do, why they say the things they say, Bill has no idea. Why won't Sarah admit how she really feels about him? And why has Helen been acting so miserable lately?

They shut the light and get in bed. The streetlights shine through the vertical blinds, allowing Bill to see. Bill violently kicks the top sheet out, allowing his feet freedom to move. Bill doesn't like the feeling of the bed closing in around him. Bill settles in, the cover tucked firmly under his chin. Even though it's hot, Bill sleeps with the cover over him. Sleeping without a cover makes him feel exposed, vulnerable. "Sure is getting hot." Helen finally breaks the silence.

"Sure is," answers Bill, as he closes his eyes. But Helen is awake, her eyes wide open.

-4-

Westbound traffic is particularly heavy this morning. Bill is in the center lane, surrounded by cars, cars in front of him, cars in back, cars on the side. The anger is festering inside him. Only the second day of summer, and he knows his whole summer is ruined. His favorite time of year, ruined. The Disagreeable Widow coming to live with them. His dopey wife moping around, acting like her best friend just died, and in the process, making Bill unhappy. Bill's sure whatever it is Helen is going through is just a phase, something that will pass. In the meantime, he'll ride out the storm.

Bill didn't even bother talking with Helen about her mother. Why get into a fight? It seems they fight about everything now. But one thing Bill would like to know is why Helen didn't say anything until the last minute. But that's not such a tough question to answer. Bill would have tried to talk her out of having her mother come live with them. Bill and Helen both know he's a master talker. It's what he does for a living. He can convince anyone of anything. And he would have convinced Helen to ship the old bat to an old age home or something.

The traffic heading eastbound is moving right along for Helen. The prospect of her mother coming to live with them is not filling her with joy either. But what can she do? She's her mother. You can't say no to her. Helen's mother can be a real pain in the neck. And it's the last thing Helen needs now, what with her mind already reeling, knowing a decision must be made soon. But what to do? Bill is the same man he always was. She still loves him. He's the perfect husband. Helen gets everything she wants. The only thing Bill can be unreasonable about is her mother. Yet he didn't yell at Helen for not telling him about her mother moving in. Hell, he didn't even talk about it. Bill is one of a kind. She knows there's no one out there better than him. But it's just not the same as it was. Just not the same.

But maybe that's the problem. It IS the same. It's been the same for years. Same house. Same job. Same Bill. Helen has changed over the years. Bill hasn't. Bill didn't have to, or he didn't want to. He thinks he knows everything. He thinks he's always right, always trying to convince Helen his way is the right way. And Bill can be really stubborn sometimes. Drives Helen crazy. His refusal to change, his rigidity, is a wall standing between Helen and Bill, a wall that's threatening to topple, taking the whole house with it.

What can it be that's bothering Helen? Must be omething at work. It can't be Bill. Bill is the same as he always was. If there was a problem with him, then it wouldn't have taken all these years of marriage for it to come out. Bill is the rock Helen can hold onto. He's always there for her. The perfect husband.

Maybe it's someone else. Maybe Helen has fallen in love with someone. Or maybe she thinks she's falling in love with someone. Or maybe she would like to fall in love with someone. Couldn't be. Bill would know if it was. He's no idiot. He could figure it out.

He just wishes Helen would tell him what's wrong, so he'd know, so he can tell her she's crazy, and convince her nothing is wrong.

The traffic is really getting to Bill. Cars are piled up on the expressway, creeping along at 5 mph, and there's nothing Bill can do about it. He just has to sit there, and move along with the others. There's no way for him to clear a path so he can get on with his life. He's a prisoner to the heavy volume or the traffic accident up ahead or to the damn 'rubber-neckers' gawking at an accident on the other side of the highway. That's what's so frustrating.

Bill can't wait to get to work. It seems he's only been happy there lately. Home has been miserable, what with Helen and the Unknown Problem, and because of it, Bill is unable to be happy in his own house. Helen is in charge of the atmosphere, in charge of who's happy and who's not. And it'll only get worse when her mother moves in. She'll spend most of her time shutting off the lights and undercooking pasta. But at work, Bill is in control of his own destiny. Once he's on the phone with a person, he's the boss. He's the best seller there at Prevail Marketing. He can do or say anything he wants.

And of course, Sarah is there. He can't stop thinking about that slip-up she made, inviting him out to The Hamptons, exposing a personal side of herself for the first time in two years. He knows exactly what she meant, even though she denied it. Why do women do that? Why can't they be like men, and just say what they feel, speak the truth? They're always being so mysterious. Bill thinks women think men like that. Well, they don't. Actually, Sarah kind of scares Bill. Here's a happily married man, and he's having these thoughts about another woman. He knows nothing will happen with Sarah, because he won't let it. That's his one saving grace. Nothing will happen unless Bill says it'll happen. Sarah can say or do anything she wants, and it doesn't matter. But then again, Sarah doesn't say or do anything. Why doesn't she? That mystery thing again, probably.

-5-

"She wants to see you." 'She' is Sally Clamp, Bill's boss. Bill was so happy when they fired Mr. Fletcher, and hired Sally. Bill gets along very well with Sally. With her, he can be himself. With Mr. Fletcher, it was all business.

"Hi, Sally," Bill says with a smile as he sits himself down on Sally's couch. Usually, Sally would smile back, and sit down on the couch next to Bill. But this time, there's no smile. She remains seated behind her desk, a file in her hand.

"We have a problem."

"A problem?" The word startles Bill. In the two year she's been here, he's never been called in for a problem. And why should he? He's the perfect employee. He outsells everyone.

"Yes. Your work."

"What's wrong with my work? I sell more than anyone out there."

"I know. That's not the problem. What it is is your tactics with the clients."

"What do you mean?" Bill is getting defensive.

"You lie to them."

Bill smiles. "Well, I wouldn't exactly call it lying. I'm trying to sell a product. So I talk it up. That's my job."

"No. Not that." Sally is annoyed with Bill's cocky smile. "We don't mind pumping up the product." She opens the file. "But what we do mind is '…just call me back the day after Labor Day, and not only will I cancel your subscription, you'll get all of your money back.' Now, you know there's no money back guarantee. And you know your not allowed to offer one, even if you tell them you'll give them the money back yourself."

The cocky smile is wiped off Bill's face. But it's replaced with a puzzled look. "How did you know I said that?"

"We tape record all the phone calls, and listen to them randomly." Sally says matter of factly.

"You do?" Bill asks, with shock in his voice.

"Sure."

"I didn't know that."

"Sure you did. It's on this employee card you signed when you were hired here." She pulls it out of the file, and shows Bill the card he signed that he never read. Sally then sheds the employer-employee stance she had to take, comes around from behind her desk, and sits besides Bill. "Listen, Bill, you can get fired for this. But I like you, and you're good. But you've got to watch what you say. All right?" Sally smiles, like she should have when Bill walked in. A stunned Bill just nods, and walks out.

One thing Bill loves about the summer is air conditioning. To him, it's the world's greatest invention. If it's hot outside, no problem, you turn on the air conditioning, and you're as cool as you want. But the air conditioning has a side effect for Bill. When he went to the doctor, fearing he had lung cancer, the doctor explained the cool air forces something in his lungs to expand, making breathing different. Not difficult, but different. Bill can actually feel each breath he takes. He can feel the air going in, can feel it move around his constricted lungs, can feel it go out. It's not asthma, as the doctor explained.

But it's the same feeling, as if someone is tightening a belt around your chest, and keeps tightening and tightening, until you feel ready to explode. The air conditioning in the office on this second day of summer is pumping out cool air.

Bill puts his hand to his chest. "We're going to lunch today." Sarah tells him. Bill just nods, and walks on.

*   *   *   *   *

Bill is quiet at lunch. He's still in a state of shock that they listen to him working. He always thought of Sally as a big sister, someone he could tell his problems to if he ever had any. But now his big sister takes on an Orwellian meaning. He doesn't feel like telling Sarah about this. But that won't be a problem, because she's not asking why he's not as talkative as usual. So in a rare turn, she's dominating the conversation, dictating what they talk about.

"They say this could be the hottest summer we've had in years."

"Oh yeah?" 'Who cares' is what Bill really wants to say. Can't she see Bill is hurting? And she's talking about the damn weather. These past couple of months, when Helen was making Bill miserable at home, he's been dropping hints to Sarah that there's some trouble. But she doesn't pick up on them. Or maybe she does, but she couldn't care less.

"Yup. They say the rough winter we had means a rough summer."

"Good." The latest in Bill's short answers.

"I plan on spending plenty of weekends at the beach this summer. I love it there. There's a certain freedom there. You walk out on the beach, and look at the ocean, and it goes on forever. There are no limits."

"Yeah."

"Here in the city," Sarah continues, not even acknowledging Bill's contribution to the conversation, "you have to act all staid and businesslike. But not at the beach. I can let my hair down, not to mention my dress."

That last bit caught Bill's attention. "Your dress?"

"Yeah. I don't have to wear these work clothes. I can wear just shorts or my bikini." The thought of Sarah in her bikini excites Bill. A warm flush goes over him. And there's a stirring in his loins. Sarah gives him that sexy look of

hers, as if she knows what she's doing to Bill. "So, you're coming out one weekend." Bill is silent for a moment. The stirring stops. Before he can answer, Sarah asks "So how are things going at home?"

Bill is taken aback. "What do you mean?"

"Just what I said. How are things going?"

"You mean with my wife?"

"Yeah."

"Fine."

"Oh really." Sarah gives Bill a sly smile, and that sexy look. The sweat begins to drip down Bill's face. It's hot in here. He asks the waiter to turn up the air conditioning. Sarah is still looking at Bill. The refreshing cold air begins to blow. Bill can feel his breath going in and out. He can feel his lungs closing in. Sarah is still looking at Bill. The belt is tightening.

-6-

"What the hell is that?" asks Bill, as he looks out of his front door, at the first piece of furniture the movers are carrying.

"That's the china closet from her dining room. Mom says it's too good not to keep."

"Who cares, as long as she keeps it in her bedroom."

"Well, it won't fit there, what with her taking her bedroom set with her."

Bill knows the answer, but he asks anyway. "So where is it going to go?"

"In the dinette area."

Knowing the answer does not stop the anger. "But it's a small area. With our small table, we can hardly walk around. Put a huge china closet in there, and the dinette area will extend beyond the line."

"What line?"

"You know what line. The line where the full pieces of wallpaper in the living room become half pieces in the dinette area, with the companion paper on the bottom."

"So."

"So?!" Bill is enraged by Helen's total lack of concern for the line. "That line tells where the dinette area ends, and the living room begins, and vice-versa. You can't just go over it. There's a natural boundary you just can't cross." Bill gives her an I-can't-believe-you-can-be-so-stupid look, while Helen blows Bill off with a you-are-such-an-idiot look.

The next piece off the truck is, or course, the big dining room table. Without saying anything, with ratchet set in hand, Bill goes into his dinette area, and disassembles his dinette set. His dinette area is now a dining room, extended several feet into the living room, several feet past the line.

The Disagreeable Widow, meanwhile, is outside, supervising the lifting and carrying of her life's possessions. She's telling the fat moving men not to drop her precious crap, not to carry the four foot high lamp in the shape of a woman by the neck. "I tooka that froma Sicily. Thatsa antique." Itsa also ugly, Bill mockingly says to himself. But there it is, next to his modern leather seafoam-green sofa. The couch used to sit comfortably against the far wall of the living room, in front of the full sheets of wallpaper. But in the new-look room, it's jammed into the corner. The dining room table can now serve as an end table.

Her mother's lovely marble French provincial coffee table is the next piece of furniture to adorn the Press household. Bill hates coffee tables. When you get up from a couch that has a coffee table in front of it, you have to do so quite carefully, so as not to hit into the table. Then you have to maneuver around it, to get to your desired destination. Without it, you just get up, and you're on your way. Now, Bill has a coffee table. Marble. French provincial. Helen's mother's. Bill looks around the room, and feels ill. His dinette area is extended over the line and into the living room. His living room is jammed with ugly furniture that does not fit in the with the decor of the room. It's filled with stuff that's not even his, stuff he doesn't like. Stuff that is being forced upon him. Bill heads upstairs, to see what horrors await him there.

When Bill gets to the top of the stairs, he hears Helen and her mother talking in the spare room—check that–her mother's room. They are talking Italian. Bill stops at the doorway and looks in. The talking stops. For the first time, Bill wishes he had listened when Helen tried to teach him Italian. What could they possibly have been talking about, with those serious looks on their faces? Maybe a woman thing, like douching or something. Her mother always had a bottle of vinegar on the dresser in her bedroom. Either she douched with it, or she made salads in the middle of the night. Bill despises the smell of vinegar. If Helen used that stuff, he'd never be able to have sex with her. Not that they have been lately, anyway.

And what about sex? There's no way Helen will want to have sex, what with her mother in the next room. Once when Bill and Helen were dating, and Helen's parents went away on vacation, Helen wouldn't even have sex in her house. They might hear the bed creaking 1,500 miles away. With her mother in the next room, Helen will remain as dry as the Sahara desert.

Bill looks around the room Helen's mother will probably, hopefully, die in. It's jammed with her bedroom set, a couple of end tables that wouldn't fit in the living room, two red velvet chairs, and about a dozen boxes filled with more junk. Nowhere is his weights and desk and computer and the little chest with the crap in it and his safe with his change on top of it. Bill looks at the two women, who have been looking at him since he stopped at the doorway. Bill takes a deep breath, turns, and walks down the hall to his bedroom. On the way, he passes his weights in the hall. He bravely walks in.

And there it is. Two rooms of furniture in one. Bill can still easily glide through the space between the bed and the dresser. But just a few feet from his side of the bed is his desk and computer, sitting there under the window. Precariously close on its left is Bill's armoire. Bill knows the answer, but he tries to open the bottom two drawers on his armoire, and of course, they only open half way, hitting into the desk. Bill's little chest with the crap in it is sitting in the middle of the room, on Helen's side of the bed. The movers apparently couldn't find a free slice of wall to put it on. The safe with his change is completely out of place, sitting on Helen's nightstand. The television stand is catty-cornered next to the desk. By putting it flush against the wall, Bill is able to squeeze his little chest between the television and Helen's dresser. Of course, now he can't see the T.V. But at least his safe with his change has now been restored to its proper home. Now, his weights. He lugs the bench-pressing bench into the room and places it next to the desk. He then carefully stacks the weights underneath it. The bar he puts in front of the bench. Now, every time he wants to work at his computer, he'll have to move the bench and the weights just to move his chair back and sit down. Bill lies down on the bed. With his left hand outstretched, he can touch the bench from the bed. Bill looks over at Helen's side of the room. It's empty, just as it was before.

"Come on down. It's time for dinner." Bill fell asleep, lying there on the bed. He's surprised he slept until dinnertime. But then he looks over at the clock, and it reads 3:15. He's only been asleep for an hour. And it's not time for dinner. Helen comes in the room. "Come on. It's time to eat."

"But it's only a quarter after three."

"You know mom always eats early on Sundays."

"But we don't, and it's our house, not her's."

"It's her house too now, and if she wants to eat early, then we'll eat early."

"But I'm not hungry. I just ate lunch a couple of hours ago."

"Well, you'll just have to force yourself."

"What are we having."

"Veal chops." Bill hates chops.

"And hard pasta?"

"Probably," Helen says, without a hint of apology in her voice. It's as if Helen is enjoying all of this. It's as if she likes having her entire house turned upside down. As if she enjoys having her mother telling her what to do, to do all the cooking, taking responsibility of the house. As if Helen is getting tired of doing it.

"You know, I'm not happy," Bill says.

"Who is?"

"You and your mother, that's who."

"First of all, mom is not happy. You think she wants to live with us, live in one room? She doesn't. It's just that she's got no where else to go. And as far as me, if you think I'm happy, then you really don't know me anymore."

"What's that supposed to mean 'then you really don't know me anymore.'" Bill says this in a more mocking tone than he intended. Helen picks up on it.

"Don't make fun of me."

"I'm not. I didn't mean it that way."

"Yes you did. Whatever I say doesn't matter. It's only what you say that counts. It's only how you feel that counts. Nothing I say is ever valid. Only your arguments are valid. And I'm getting sick of it. Because I know how I feel. And how I feel is important. And how I feel is right." Helen starts to cry as she rambles. "And I'm not going to let you change my mind anymore, or say what I feel doesn't count, because it does."

"Why are you crying? Of course what you say counts."

Helen gets more hysterical. "You don't care what I think. You don't. It's only what you think that counts. Well not any more.

Not any more." Helen runs into the bathroom, without giving Bill the chance to convince Helen that what she feels is valid, that it's not only what he feels that counts. Bill is confused. He's not exactly sure what Helen is talking about. So he goes downstairs to eat some hard pasta and some bad chops.

"Whatsa alla the yelling about?"

"Nothing. Helen's upset about something."

"Whatdya say to her?"

All of a sudden, it's his fault. "Nothing. Did you hear me yelling up there? It was all her."

"Listen. Can I tella you something?"

"What."

"Helen, she'sa going through a harda time. She won't tella me what it is. So be nice to her."

"I'm always nice." Bill growls. "I'm letting her do anything she wants. Besides, everything is fine. Helen is not going through anything." Maybe the old bat is smarter than she looks.

"Alla right. I'm just telling you to be nice to her."

"And I'm telling you, I appreciate the concern, but everything is fine, believe me."

"I don'ta think so, but alla right."

In the fight for the last word, Bill says "Don't worry."

"Alla right." Bill is about to continue the battle but Helen comes down the stairs.

"I'm sorry," is all she says.

"That's all right," Bill and the Disagreeable Widow say in unison.

The house is sweltering. Helen's mother made them shut off the central air conditioning. "I don'ta likea it." Bill tries to explain to her that this is no barn somewhere in Sicily. This is America, and here, there is air conditioning. But she doesn't like it, preferring to sweat and stick on the leather couch.

Bill would never admit it, but he is sort of relieved that the air conditioning is off for a while. For the first time today, he can breathe. The warm, stagnant air has opened up his lungs, like a great weight has been lifted off his chest. Helen's mother lights up a cigarette. If she puts a burn hole in the couch, Bill will kill her. Soon, the entire downstairs reeks of smoke. It hangs in the air. Even after she puts it out, it's still there. It'll always be there.

Helen shuts the kitchen light, and joins Bill and her mother in the living room. So Bill must get up, and turn the light back on. As he walks back to his chair, carefully maneuvering around the damn coffee table, he looks at the two women on the couch. Now, it's two against one. It'll be two of them shutting off the lights, two of them cooking hard pasta, two of them cooking chops, two women against him.

Women always need a compatriot, don't they? It's become a cliche already, but they always go to the bathroom in pairs, don't they? Women are always talking amongst themselves, giggling, conspiring against men. There seems to be this secret bond among women. They always stick together. Men, on the other hand, are alone. Alone to fight the world's battles. Alone to the bathroom. A man has no one to count on except himself. He has no secret bond with other men. The only secret bond a man has is with a woman, and this woman already has a secret bond with the other members of her gender. So the man is alone. Bill fears being alone. He's alone in his battle against his wife and her mother.

"You know mom likes the light off."

"But she knows I like the light on. And it's my house."

"It's not your house, it's our house. All three of ours."

"Well, I want the light on, she wants it off. So what do we do?"

"Well, I'll cast the third vote." Helen thinks for a second. A short second. "Off." Helen gets up, glides past the coffee table like she's been doing it her whole life, and flips off the light. Bill is fuming. He considers leaving, but this is his house, he's the king, he's the general, and he's not going to let two women drive the king from his throne. So he'll sit in the damn dark.

Bill flips on the T.V. The Mets are playing a rare Sunday night game. The Disagreeable Widow says something in Italian to Helen, and Helen says "Mom doesn't want to watch baseball."

All of a sudden, she can't speak English. "Well, what does she want to watch?"

"There's a movie on HBO. 'Sleeping with the Enemy.' She wants to watch that."

"So let her watch it in her room."

"You know there's no cable upstairs."

"But I want to watch the Mets."

"Well, we don't." The 'we' stings Bill. Helen used to like watching the Mets. Bill got her interested in it when they first started dating. But lately, her interest has waned. "Why don't you watch in the bedroom?"

"Because I don't want to."

"Yeah, why don'ta you go upastairs. You cana turn alla the lights ona you want." She meant this as a joke, but she is the only one laughing. Again, Bill considers leaving. But he refuses to be thrown out of his castle. So he gets up from his chair, hits his leg on the damn French provincial coffee table, and heads upstairs.

Watching television in the newly redecorated bedroom is no easy task. Half of the screen is hidden behind the desk. So either Bill can watch only half the game, or he can sit on the floor on the side of the T.V., and see the whole screen, or he can take a third option: lift the T.V. off the stand, lift the stand out of the corner and put it in the space between the bed and Helen's dresser. Then, when the game is over, Bill can reverse the process. He chooses this option, because it affords him the best look at the screen.

Baseball truly is the thinking man's sport. Some call it slow and plodding. But Bill loves it, because during those slow times is when the thinking comes in. The strategy. The manager can plan his means of attack. Whether to have his pitcher throw a fastball or a curve. Whether to hit and run. Or whether to try the suicide squeeze. That's Bill's favorite play: the suicide squeeze. In the instant the pitch is thrown, and the batter squares around, you know what's coming. And it's so exciting seeing that runner take off down the line, the pitcher charging, the catcher getting out of his crouch, the batter focusing on that baseball. But what bothers Bill is that you have your mind made up to call for the suicide squeeze, but sometimes the opposition screws you up by calling for a pitchout, easily throwing your runner out at home. That's the one bad thing about baseball: the other side is thinking too, coming up with its own plan of attack. And sometimes, their plan is better than yours, and you lose, through no fault of your own. It's just that the other side played the game better than you did.

-7-

The alarm goes off at 6:00, as it does every day from Monday through Friday. But unlike past weekdays, the house is already brimming with activity. Helen is not in bed next to him, as usual. He can smell coffee brewing downstairs, something Helen usually does after Bill leaves, since he doesn't drink coffee. And someone is in the bathroom. Bill listens to the news, as usual. The smiling newswoman tells us all about the sensational divorce trial between the billionaire and his wife. She's saying all sorts of things about him, making him look like the biggest beast since the Jurassic era. Of course she never mentions all the diamonds and furs and furniture and clothes he bought her over the years with his inherited billions. Of course not. All it takes is a few wild statements by a woman to make a man's life miserable. And we all have to listen to the crap. But Bill is not too worried about him. He's sure he's got his own ideas for victory.

At 6:19, like he's done everyday for years, Bill drags himself out of bed. He kicks the big toe of his right foot on his barbell as he takes his first step. Bill just winces. He then has to move the television stand from the space between the bed and the dresser, where he left it last night. He walks towards the bathroom. The door is closed. He hears someone inside. He turns the knob.

Locked. Walking up the stairs with a cup of coffee in her hands, Helen informs Bill that her mother is in there. Bill explains how he needs to get into the bathroom now, that his whole morning is mapped out so as to give him maximum time in bed. Throw off the process by just a few minutes, and Bill will be late for work. Helen just shrugs. Bill walks back to the bedroom, and sits on the edge of the bed, waiting. Helen takes off her nightshirt, and looks at her nude body in the full length mirror. She cups her hands under her small breasts. She lets out a sigh. So does Bill. Just once, he'd like to bury his face in a set of huge tits. He looks at Helen again. She's still got bigger ones than Sarah, although he wouldn't mind burying his face there, either.

Finally, the Disagreeable Widow comes out of the bathroom. Bill glances over at the clock. 6:28. Nine minutes behind schedule. He goes into the bathroom, and locks the door. The bathroom stinks like Helen's mother. He looks around, and sees a new addition to his bathroom. It's some sort of after-shower body splash. Bill opens it up and takes a whiff, and is immediately repelled. Smells just like Helen's mother, just like her bathroom. Bill brushes his teeth. But the horrible flavor has been there so much longer than usual, he thinks he has to brush twice just to get rid of it. He drops his pants, and sits on the toilet. But just as his bottom hits the seat, he jumps back up. Bill takes a piece of toilet paper, and wipes off the seat, so he won't get any of Helen's mother's germs. Just as he's about to step into the shower, Helen bangs. She needs the bathroom. Too fucking bad, Bill thinks, and ignores her. Bill thinks a second before getting in. Helen's mother was just in there, showering off her dirt. And now, he'll be stepping where her dirty water just was. So he takes the removable shower-head off, and cleans off the tub. Then, he steps in. After washing his hair, Bill picks up the soap, the same soap she used to wash herself in her private area that is so filthy, it must be douched to keep clean. The soap in Bill's hand makes him feel ill. He needs a bar of soap just to wash off the bar of soap. So he steps out of the shower dripping wet, to get his own brand new bar. After he's done, Bill takes his bar of soap, wraps it back up in the paper, and puts it back under the sink. There it is, his own personal bar of soap, in his own little hiding place. Bill smiles for the first time this morning. Helen bangs again. Bill would like to take his sweet time, just to annoy Helen. But he knows he must make up for lost time, so he does his hair and his contacts quickly, rinses his mouth out yet once again, and vacates the bathroom. He sneers at Helen as he passes her in the doorway. He also sneers at her mother as he passes the closed door to what once was his spare bedroom, which once was home to his weights and desk and computer and the little chest with his crap in it and the safe with his change on top of it.

Bill enters the new home to his stuff. He maneuvers around the obstacles, and gets to his sock drawer. The drawer only opens half way, of course, what with the desk there. So Bill must fish around for his tan socks, throwing back the black ones and the grey ones and the blue ones before finding the tan ones. For today's outfit, he picks his tan pants to match with his tan socks, his light brown shirt, and the tie with the light brown and the tan in it. Bill's father kids him that it's a good tie, because you could drop food on it, and no one would know.

Bill is now four minutes behind schedule. So he rushes around, trying to get ready. He picks up his wallet, keys, and Ray-Bans, and is all set to go. He bangs on the bathroom door to tell Helen he is leaving. She's thrilled.

Downstairs, he sees Helen's mother, sitting on the sofa, drinking coffee, and smoking a cigarette. "I heara you rushing around. Why don'ta you get upa earlier."

"I'll have to do that from now on."

"Dida you forgeta anything? Usually whena you rush around, you forgeta something."

"No, I didn't forget anything," Bill says, not trying to hide his resentment.

"Are you sure?"

"Yes, I'm sure."

"Alla right." She says this in that if-you-say-so tone. Bill looks at his watch. This little conversation has now put him six minutes behind schedule. He'll let her get the last word again, only because he's late.

Summertime traffic is unusually light. Today, the expressway actually lives up to its name. Bill is breezing through, easily making up the time Helen's mother cost him. 'Dida you forgeta anything'? As if Bill is a child. And why is Helen constantly looking at herself in the mirror? She's starting to lose a little too much weight. You can see her ribs. And her face is drawn. She doesn't look healthy. But more important to Bill, her breasts are disappearing. She better start eating again. But what difference does it make? Helen's hands are the only ones that have touched her breasts in weeks.

As Bill approaches the toll, it hits him that he has no tokens left. And he forgot to take change from his safe because he was rushing around, trying to get back on schedule. But that's all right, he's probably got enough change in the car. He gets to the toll machine, opens his ashtray, and counts out the change. All he has is $3.20. He panics. He looks in his rear view mirror. Cars have lined up behind him. They begin to honk. Bill puts his car in reverse, and everyone must back up to let him out. Damn Helen's mother, Bill thinks, she's making me look like an idiot. Damn Helen and her fucking problems. Damn Sarah, too. Damn them all.

-8-

"Mrs. Berkowitz. It's Bill Press calling you from Empire Bank MasterCard. How are you on this fine day?"

"I already have a MasterCard," the cranky old woman answers back.

"I'm sure you do. Who in this day and age doesn't? But you don't have the Empire Bank MasterCard, do you?"

"No. What's the difference? A MasterCard is a MasterCard."

In mock shock, Bill says "A MasterCard is a MasterCard? I'm glad I'm not on a speakerphone, because people would be jumping out of windows if they heard that. What you just said is blasphemy in the banking world."

"Blasphemy," Mrs. Berkowitz says sarcastically. "I see right through your little game. I'm supposed to ask you all about your stupid card, and then you go into your sales pitch, and before I know it, I bought one. Right?" Bill is speechless. The 'blasphemy' thing usually works. So Mrs. Berkowitz answers for him. "Right." And she hangs up.

Bill takes a moment to recover from his blow. He doesn't mind not making a sale. Hell, there are more misses than hits in this business, anyway. But he usually gets further than this. So, after taking a moment to compose himself, Bill calls the next number on his list.

"Mrs. Nelson. It's Bill Press, from Empire Bank MasterCard. I have one word to say to you. Control."

"Control?" a baffled Mrs. Nelson asks.

"Control."

"What about it?"

"Control is the most important thing a person can have in their life."

"Go on."

She's taking the bait perfectly. "And what's the most important thing in the world?"

"Love?"

"Guess again."

"Your health?"

"Try again."

"Children?"

Mrs. Nelson is truly an idiot. "Money."

"Money's not the most important thing."

"Sure it is. But most people don't like to admit it. Let's face it, money is everything. It dictates where you live, what kind off food you eat, what kind of car you drive, what kind of clothes you wear. Money DOES make the world go round."

"I guess you're right."

"Of course I'm right."

"So what does this have to do with control?" Students at tele-marketing college could use Mrs. Nelson to build up their morale.

"Well, wouldn't you like to control the most important thing in the world."

"I guess."

"You guess?"

"I mean yes."

Bill is feeling better about himself, and about life in general. He takes back that 'Damn Sarah.' "And the way to control your money is with the Empire Bank MasterCard."

"How would a credit card help me control my money?"

Bill uses the always effective technique of feigning insult. "You insult me and the Empire Bank MasterCard by calling it simply a credit card. It's much more than that. The Empire Bank MasterCard is your key to the world."

"How's that?" Where was she when Bill was selling Amway?

"Do you know how many businesses take the Empire Bank MasterCard?"

"How many?"

Bill doesn't know either. He's about to make up some ridiculous figure like 750,000,000, when he sees in his head a tape machine rolling, recording every word he is saying. "Um, I don't know. But I'll bet it's plenty."

"Oh." The woman seems genuinely disappointed, as if she enjoyed the con game Bill has been playing, as if she enjoyed the sweet talk her husband never gives her anymore. With the spell broken, she asks, "What is the interest rate?"

In the past, Bill has lied about this. He'd always say something like 11%. The interest rate is on the bottom of the bill, in small numbers. No one ever sees it. And if they ever called back, Bill would have said the rate went up in the time he quoted it. But with Big Sister listening, he blurts out the truth. "19.5%"

"That's quite high, isn't it? Most bank cards are around 11% or 12%."

"That's true. But think about the reputation of Empire Bank."

"I've never heard of it."

"Oh, well, in these days of bad-news-is-the-only-news, that's a plus. It means the bank has never been involved in any scandals."

"Or, it's such a small, penny-ante bank, that it can't possibly provide the services of a large bank."

That's the truth. "Sure, one could look at it that way," Bill stammers. He knows it's all over. "Can I send you an application?" Bill asks, already knowing the answer.

"No thanks, but it was nice talking to you."

"Yeah, right." He throws his headset down in disgust. He buries his head in his hands, trying to figure out what's going wrong. He picks his head up, and Sarah's there.

"We're eating Chinese today." She walks away. Damn her.

-9-

Sarah invited Bill, and presumably 'his wife' out to her parents house in The Hamptons for this July 4th weekend. Bill wanted to go, even if it meant bringing Helen. But of course, Helen said no, that it wouldn't be right leaving mom all alone on a holiday weekend. Like it would kill her to be alone. That's the whole reason Helen insisted on having her mother live with them: so her mother wouldn't be alone. Well, life is tough. Sometimes people are left alone. Like when Helen's old man up and died, he left her mother alone. And instead of dealing with it and taking it like an adult, she's got to move in with her daughter, so she won't be alone.

Bill has little sympathy for Helen's mother. Let her be alone. Yet being alone is Bill's biggest fear. He secretly hopes he dies before Helen, so he won't be alone. On the days Sarah is out sick or on vacation, he doesn't even take a lunch. He'd rather go hungry than to sit in a restaurant alone, and have people look at him, thinking what a loser, he has to go to lunch alone. Bill looks at these people, and sure he thinks they are losers, but he also envies them, the way they sit alone, reading the newspaper, eating lunch, and not minding it at all. There must be something in these people, some kind of inner strength, that allows them to be alone. Bill wishes he had that inner strength. He wishes he knew what that inner strength is.

So Bill will spend this three day holiday weekend at home, in the hot sweltering city. That smiling newswoman said on Friday that it would be so hot this weekend, you won't even need a match to light the fireworks. And they pay her for this.

Bill really isn't too upset about being at home. It would have been frustrating to see Sarah prancing around in her bikini, while his wife with the incredible shrinking breasts sits besides him. He's just glad he's not at work.

Things have been going pretty poorly there. His sales have plummeted since he started watching every word he says. This past week, he's been the worst seller at Prevail Marketing. And his boss Sally Clamp hasn't been shy about telling him so. She said her bosses have been asking questions about him, like why the best seller has become the worst seller. She covered for him, making up some phony story about problems at home. But she said if things don't pick up, they will force her to fire him.

So this Independence Day holiday is sure to be a fun one for Bill. His job is hanging from a thread. The Disagreeable Widow is living with him. His wife is getting more miserable by the day. And the woman he may like more than he should is in The Hamptons, probably getting laid by some guy that should be Bill. Let the fireworks begin.

-10-

Each year, Helen begs Bill to take her to the big fireworks show. But Bill always complains about the traffic, and how he has to go to work the next day, and he doesn't want to get home late. And why should he have to stand around with a million other idiots looking up into the sky, saying ooh and aah. So they never go. But this year, Helen didn't even bother asking. So Bill offered, figuring it might cheer her up. Plus, the Fourth falls out on a Sunday, and everybody has the Monday off, so Bill can get home late. But still, Helen doesn't want to go. He offers one last time, on the morning of the Fourth.

"No."

"Why?"

"I just don't want to go, all right?"

"No, it's not all right. Every year, you want to go. And now, that I'm telling you I'm willing to go, you don't want to."

"Oh. Just because you want to go means we have to go. So all those years that I wanted to go doesn't matter. As long as you want to go, we'll go. As long as the king deems it agreeable to go means we must go. Well, no more 'yes master' for me."

"What are you talking about, 'yes master?'"

"That's what I've been saying all these years." Helen starts to cry. She always does this when she rambles. "Whenever you said no, it was no. Whenever you said yes, it was yes. I never got what I wanted. I let you win all of those stupid arguments."

Now Bill's ears perk up. "What do you mean you let me win? I won those arguments with clear, concise, logical thinking."

"And by twisting my words and feelings around until you got me to say and feel what you wanted me to say and feel."

"That's not true. I just laid out all of the facts, and presented them in such a way that proved my way of thinking was the right way of thinking."

"You treated me just like one of those idiots you used to sell crap to. The ones you used to laugh about, how you were able to con people into buying stuff. And I am using the past tense on purpose, because lately it seems you can't sell anything to anyone. You can't get anyone to think like you want them to think." Bill falls silent. What can he say? She's right. Only it hurts hearing it. The silence lasts for what seems like an eternity.

When Bill was a kid, he'd get these pimples, like most kids did. They would start out red, but he just knew they would turn white. They would build and build, until he had to give them a squeeze, letting white crap shoot all over the mirror. The unpleasant act would relieve the pressure. It must be done, to make those pimples go away. So like a pimple, this thing with Bill and Helen has come to a head, and Helen must give it that final, inevitable squeeze.

"I think I want to move out for a while."

Bill nods his head in silence. It's not a stunned silence, because he saw this coming. But it's kind of a numb silence, as if he can't believe he's actually having this conversation, that this is actually happening to him. This happens to other people, not Bill Press. In fact, just a few months earlier, Helen asked him why so many marriages are breaking up, and their's is not. Well, Bill put on that air of superiority he seems to wear so well, and said because most people are stupid, and they are not.

Now Helen begins to tell the reasons for this. She tosses out every cliche ever spoken on big fat Oprah's show. I love you, but I'm not in love with you. What the hell does that mean, anyway? It's something that women say. You never hear a man say that. We've grown apart. That's a load of crap. Another thing women say when they want to dump a guy. We just don't work anymore. What are we, a colony of ants? And the kicker, she doesn't have to tell Bill that their sex life isn't what it once was. That's true. Helen hasn't allowed Bill to touch her for months. But he remembers how it once was. He remembers when they were still in college. Helen would call her mother, just to make sure she was at work. Then, they'd go into Helen's room and lie down on her small bed. They'd give each other deep, passionate kisses. Bill would kiss Helen's neck, and nibble on her ear, causing Helen to giggle. He would unbutton her shirt, and undo her bra, and gently lick Helen's nipples. They would instantly harden. Then, kissing her torso as he did it, Bill would make his way to Helen's pants. He would undo the button, unzip the zipper, and peel them off, panties included. Then he would delve his tongue deeply into Helen. She would arch her back in pleasure. Bill remembers the sweet taste, and that musty, sexy odor. Bill would stand up, to take his clothes off. Helen would sit on the edge of the bed, and stroke Bill. Gently at first, then harder. She'd lick him, first at the bottom, then all the way to the head. Bill's legs would quiver. Then she'd take him fully in her mouth, until Bill was ready to explode. She'd swallow some, and the rest would drip onto her body. Helen would rub it all over her breasts as they lay back down on the bed. They would continue to play with each other, until Bill was ready to go again. He'd get on top, his hands on the bed, his arms straight, hovering over Helen, looking into her eyes, as he entered her. Helen would let out a sigh, and a groan of pleasure as he entered all the way. Bill would slowly lie down on top of Helen as they pumped in unison. Bill would look into Helen's eyes, and see all of her love and passion. He would reach down, and gently massage her. He would push harder and harder and harder until Helen would scream in ecstasy. Then he would continue to go in and out, until he would reach that same ecstasy. Then, they would hold each other, both of them saying how much they love the other. But that was so many years ago.

-II-

Helen throws the bag on the bed and unzips it. She fills it up with the essentials. Her blouses, her skirts, her dresses, her pants, her underwear, her bras, her sexy lingerie. She stops, and looks at her black garter belt and red teddy in the suitcase. She takes them out, and places them back in her drawer. She stops again, and puts them back in the suitcase. What will she need them for? She puts them back in the drawer. The black garter and black bra were Bill's favorites. Sometimes she'd greet him at the door after work wearing the garter, and they'd make love all night. She puts them back in the suitcase. She might use them. Who knows? Helen looks at herself in the mirror. She's still young. Early 30's. And she still looks good. Sure, she's lost some weight recently, but who wouldn't when they're trying to make a decision about the rest of their life. Who could have an appetite? Who could sleep? Bill could, that's who. He's so damn perfect, nothing effects him. All he did was just nod his head when she told him she was leaving. He showed no emotion. He didn't even care. He didn't even ask her to stay. Not that it would have made any difference, because her mind was made up. But maybe if he did seem upset, she would have stayed. No, her mind was made up. He thinks he's so great, like he's better than everyone else. What he thinks is right, and what everybody else thinks is wrong. Her breasts look so small. Bill likes big tits. What did he marry her for? He was always kidding around that Helen should get breast implants. But he wasn't kidding. Well good, let the perfect guy go out and find his big breasted perfect model with the tits and the blue eyes and the full lips and the long legs and the flat stomach. Let them be very happy together. Mr. and Mrs. Perfect. Bill really is a good guy. No, he's a great guy. All of the qualities Bill had when Helen married him are still there. So why is she leaving? She throws her vibrator into the suitcase and zips it up. It's been her best friend lately.

That, and Jerry.

"Whatsa going on upa there?" Helen's mother asks as Bill walks down the stairs and settles into his chair, but first making sure he doesn't hit his leg on the damn coffee table.

"Helen's leaving."

"She's what?!"

"Leaving."

"Why?"

"Why. How do I know?" ·

"Well, aren't youa going to stopa her."

"It's out of my hands. There's nothing I can do," as Bill turns on the Mets game.

"Listena to me. I knowa you guys havea been having troubles. But she shouldn'ta leave. You got to stop her. She'sa waiting for you to stop her."

"No she's not. Her mind's made up. She's leaving."

"I thinka you'rea wrong."

"Of course you think I'm wrong. No one's right except for you." Bill actually feels a little bad about saying this, so he changes his tone. "Well, I think I know your daughter a little better than you do."

"Fine. You do whatever you think is right. But I thinka you'rea wrong."

"You've told me."

"You should go talka to her."

"I'll handle this the way I think best."

"Fine."

"Good."

"Alla right."

"Fine." This never-ending battle for the last word would continue, but Helen comes walking down the stairs, bag in tow.

"I'm sorry mom, I've got to move out for a while."

"Where area you going to go?" Bill looks up. He hasn't thought about where Helen is going to go. He'd say her mother's house, but her mother's house is his house. So the answer to this question will interest him greatly.

"To a friend's house."

"What friend?" asks Bill.

"A friend from work."

"Who?"

"A friend."

"I want a name."

"I don't feel like telling you." Bill wants to put his foot down, and refuse to let her leave until she tells him where she is going. But he's afraid of the answer. So he just tells her good, go then. She kisses her mother goodbye. She looks at Bill, who still hasn't gotten out of his chair. She walks out of the front door. Her mother watches her walk to the car. Bill finally gets up, and goes to the door to watch. Helen puts the bag in her trunk, starts up the car, and takes off. Bill looks out at the empty space. His greatest fear is realized. He's alone. He looks down at his mother in law. She looks up. He's not alone. She's here.

PART II

-12-

"Why are you crying?," Jerry asks Helen as Helen walks into what will be her new home for the time being, maybe for a long time being.

"Why am I crying," Helen answers in a mocking tone.

"Yeah, why are you crying?"

"Because I just left my husband."

"But I thought that's what you wanted to do. I thought it would make you happy. If anyone should be crying, it's him, the bastard. You shouldn't be crying for something you yourself did."

Helen has to laugh. "That sounds like something he would say."

"Bite your tongue, or on second thought, let me do it for you." Jerry makes a move towards Helen, but Helen signals to stop.

"Not right now. I'm upset."

"Yeah, and I still don't see why."

"Women are very sensitive. We cry for no apparent reason."

"Hey, you don't have to tell me that."

"Sometimes I think I do."

Jerry looks at Helen's bags, where she left them in the middle of the living room. "Don't leave your bags in the middle of the room. Bring them into the bedroom."

"Fine." Fine. That's a word Helen picked up from Bill. Fine. Everything was always fine. She leaves, he says fine. Helen brings her bags into the bedroom and sits down on the bed. Everything was not fine. If everything was fine, why did Helen have to turn to Jerry? Jerry was always looking at her at work. Helen never paid it any mind. She was a married woman, not to mention the fact she wasn't attracted to Jerry in the least bit. But Jerry kept making those sexual jokes, and there was the lure of the unknown, but still Helen was not interested. But then there was that one day...Jerry calls from the living room, breaking Helen's fond memory.

"Hey, make us some tea."

"Fine." So Helen walks to the kitchen to make the tea.

"So how did he take it?" Jerry calls into the kitchen.

"He was all right, too all right if you ask me. I told him, and he just nodded his head. Just kept nodding his head. As if he was too perfect to show some emotion."

"Did you tell him about me?"

"No. I just told him I was going to a friend's house. He wouldn't understand. And he just let me go. I have to wonder how much he still loves me. If he loves me, he shouldn't have just let me walk out the door, without knowing where I'm going. I could be living in the street for all he knows. But that's the way he is. When it comes right down to it, that's all he cares about. Himself. Maybe he has someone else. Maybe that's why he was happy to see me go.

Maybe he's got some big breasted woman he's fucking."

"Well, you know what they say, 'what's good for the goose...'"

"Shut up." Helen walks into the living room with the teapot and two cups. She pours one for Jerry, and then one for herself.

"I'll bet he knows about us."

"No way."

"Why?"

"You don't know him like I do. He's really kinky sexually. He used to bring up the idea of a third partner all the time. Not that he'd be thrilled that I'm doing it with you without him. But he'd at least want to take part once before divorcing me, to satisfy his sick desires. So now it looks like I'm divorcing him. Who would've thought it? He really is a great guy."

Jerry is angry. Jerry doesn't like to talk about Bill, won't even say Bill's name. "So why don't you go back to him then, if he's such a great guy."

"Because I don't love him anymore. I love you."

But Jerry is still angry. "Show me how much you love me." They've played this game a thousand times before. Helen talks about Bill. Jerry gets angry. Then Helen must reassure Jerry that it's Jerry, and not Bill, who's the love of her life. Helen thinks it's just Jerry's way of getting sex when Jerry is horny and she is not. But Helen doesn't feel like playing the game right now. She needs to be taken care of. Can't Jerry see that? Jerry and Bill are so very different, yet they are alike in so many ways. But even though it's the last thing she wants to do, Helen must play the game. She left her husband just an hour ago, but there's Helen sliding off Jerry's pants, and burying her head between Jerry's legs.

-13-

The alarm clock goes off at exactly 6:19. Except for him, his bed is empty. Helen even took her pillow. It's the saddest thing you'd ever want to see—a queen size bed, with one pillow. And to compound matters, his mother in law insists on making the bed after he gets up. Bill and Helen never made their bed. Why bother? They were just going to mess it up the next night. So now you see a made bed, with a lone pillow, just begging to be messed up. But Bill is alone now. There will be no messing of the bed. Bill wishes his mother in law would stay out of his bedroom. He doesn't like anyone else in his space, touching his bed and pillow. Who knows? Maybe he didn't wash her hands after she douched, and she's getting the discharge that spilled out of her filthy vagina all over his pillow, where Bill's head lies 8 or 9 hours a day.

And what about the Disagreeable Widow? Why is she still here? Why doesn't Helen get custody of her? She's her responsibility, not Bill's. If she leaves, Bill can get all of his stuff out of his bedroom, and back where it belongs, so he can regain a little order in his life.

It's Tuesday. It's a funny thing. On Friday, Bill dreaded Tuesday. It would mean he'd have to go back to work after what he was hoping could be a pleasant three day weekend. He's still under close scrutiny because of his poor work performance. And he'd have to hear Sarah's stories about frolicking in her bikini in The Hamptons with some guy. But here it is Tuesday, and Bill is relishing it. Being cooped up with the Disagreeable Widow for the past day and a half has been no picnic, what with her constantly saying Where isa Helen? Why don'ta you go out anda find her insteada watchinga T.V? Eata your pasta. Finish your dinner. It's like living with his mother, only worse. It's Helen's mother.

And Bill also can't wait to tell Sarah what happened. He's finally a free man, free to do what he wants. Sarah is free to finally reveal her true feelings for Bill. One of the first thoughts in his mind when Helen said she was leaving was about Sarah. This both excited and bothered Bill. How much could he love his wife if the first thought in his mind was Sarah? That's one reason he didn't beg Helen to stay. Sure, part of him wanted her to stay. But the other part said good, go. I've got other fish to fry, as it were.

Bill gets out of bed. He almost has to peel his bare back off his sheet, since he sweat so much during the night. 'I don't likea to sleep with the air condition.' Bill looks at himself in the mirror. He looks horrible. But what would you expect, after just a few hours of sleep. Bill tossed and turned all night. Bill doesn't like sleeping alone. He could never sleep as a child. And it just got worse as a teenager. But after getting married, he was able to sleep like a log. Just the feeling of someone else beside him, to take care of him, put his mind at easy.

Bill opens up the cabinet, and takes out his secret bar of soap. Every time he does this, he smiles, as if he's got something that no one else knows about. It's as if his bar of soap is the only pure thing left, the only thing untouched, the only thing not spoiled for him. To Bill, his bar of soap is the only thing right in his world. It's there every day, to clean off the dirt and grime this cruel, cruel world heaps upon him.

Bill leaves the bathroom, and sees his mother in law's door is still closed. Good, maybe she's still sleeping, maybe he won't have to see her this morning. But those happy thoughts fly out the open window which is allowing the stifling hot air into the room, when he sees his bed has been made. She's up and around. Bill shuts the door, but her presence is still in the room. Bill messes up the bed, and it makes him feel better. For his big day with Sarah, he picks his white shirt to make the slight tan he acquired while lying on his deck this weekend stand out, his teal pants, and his tie with the teal flowers.

Bill walks downstairs, and his mother in law is sitting among the clutter, drinking coffee, smoking a cigarette. "I madea you breakafast."

Bill sighs. "You know I don't eat breakfast." God, how he hates her.

"You shouldn'ta go out on an empty stomach. Especially in thisa heat. You coulda get, how do you say, lighthead?"

Bill doesn't tell her the correct word. He doesn't want her to get too smart. "Well, I'll tell you. For 30-some years I've been going out without breakfast. And I never got 'lighthead.'"

His mother in law knows she used the wrong word, and she knows Bill is making fun of her. She's hurt, so she doesn't answer. Bill doesn't pick up on this as he walks out of the house with a self-serving smirk on his face. All he knows is he got the last word.

It is awfully hot outside. Only about 7:15 in the morning, and already it must be 85 degrees. Bill gets to his car, starts it up, and quickly turns on the air conditioning. But instead of cold air blowing on his face, all he hears is a hiss. On all days for the air conditioning to go, why today? Annoyed, and already sweating from the walk to the car, Bill rolls down his window, then leans over to open up the passenger side window. The cross ventilation creates nothing. There's no wind, so the air just hangs there in the car, like his mother in law's smoke hangs in the living room, over-seeing everything.

Bill's hope that getting on the highway will get the air moving proves to be a disappointment. The moment he enters, there's bumper to bumper traffic. He flicks on the all news station to find out what's going on. Bill listens through the weathercaster telling him its going to be hot today (no kidding), but then hears nothing about his particular route to work during the traffic report. He never hears about his route, as if there's a more important route in this damn city than his! Bill figures it must he something like a 'jack-knifed tractor-trailer.' Just exactly what that means is a mystery to Bill, but he assumes he'll find out today.

If only it was that simple to figure out the mystery of the women. Bill wishes someone could point it out to him, just like people will be pointing to that tractor-trailer, and saying to their carpool buddy "so that's what they mean when they say 'jack-knifed.'" And then they'll have a good laugh like the morons they are. Why can't someone say to Bill "so this is what women are all about. This is why they do the things they do." He's thought about this a lot lately, ever since Helen's problems began. And why did they begin? They were the happiest couple in the world. And then just like that, boom, Helen's not happy. It sure is getting hot in the car. Bill is moving at just a few miles an hour, when he's moving at all. The fumes from the bus on the right of Bill's car are making him sick to his stomach. He leans over, to roll up the pas-senger window. That makes the bus smell go away, but makes it that much hotter in the car.

Bill turns on the traffic report once again, but still, no mention of his route. Not knowing what's going on frustrates Bill. It's not as though he can take another highway into work, but he just likes to know what's going on. He doesn't like the fact that some unknown force out of his control is having such a drastic effect on his life. There are so many things out of his control these days, Bill wants to be able to control what little he can. Now, he can't control what time he gets to work. And he can't even control the temperature in his car. The sweat is rolling down Bill's face. He scrounges around in the glove compartment for a napkin to wipe his face off, but he can't find one. The bus is no longer on his right, so he leans over and rolls the window back down. Leaning over made all the blood rush to Bill's head, so when he gets up, his vision is unfocused. It takes a second before his eyes adjust. Damn heat.

One thing he knows about women: they are always right. When he used to argue with Helen, most of the time he knew she was right. But he's smarter than her, and was able to trick her into thinking he was right, without her even knowing what he was doing. Men are smarter than women, that's why they control the world. So why are women always right, then?

Now traffic comes to a complete halt. That bus is sitting in the center lane, on Bill's right, spewing those fumes straight into Bill's car. Now it's smoke from the bus hanging in Bill's car. He breathes in those fumes, and it makes him feel sick. He feels like throwing up, although he knows there's nothing in his stomach to come out. Good thing he didn't eat his mother in law's stupid breakfast. He separates his sweaty back from the vinyl seat, and leans over to shut the window, to shut out those fumes. When he gets up his eyes are unfocused, the way they were before. But it doesn't clear up. He can feel his head moving about, like a balloon blowing in the wind. The women are always right, Bill thinks as he passes out.

Bill feels his head moving about again, this time shaking violently, as he tries to get away from the smelling salts the paramedic is holding under his nose. Now he knows how a boxer feels, when his manager breaks open that unknown stick, and the fighter suddenly wakes up. That usually happens at the end of the bout. But for Bill, his fight is just beginning.

"How do you feel?" asks the paramedic.

"Fine," Bill tells her.

"You passed out." No shit, Bill would like to answer. But she is only trying to help, so he just nods his head. "It's this heat. It's unbearable. And I'll bet you didn't eat anything this morning."

Damn it, they all know. "That's got nothing to do with it," he snaps. "I never eat. It's just that my air conditioner is broken, and this damn traffic." Bill looks up and finds the damn traffic ahead of his is gone. Behind him, though, is traffic, caused by him. Bill feels badly, holding all these people up. "Listen, thanks, I've got to go. I'm late for work."

"I wouldn't go to work if I were you. I suggest you just go right back home and lie down."

Bill would like to do that, but it means spending the day with his the Disagreeable Widow. Besides, he's looking forward to seeing Sarah. "Thanks, but I'm fine." He finishes off the last of the orange juice she gave him, gets back in his car, and takes off. He turns on the traffic report, and finally he hears a report about his route. The jack-knifed tractor trailer that has been causing those earlier problems has been cleared (damn, he missed it) but there's another tie-up, because of a stalled four wheeler in the left lane. Bill wonders what that's all about, not realizing it's all about him.

By the time Bill gets to work a half an hour late, the shirt that was completely drenched with his perspiration is almost dried, but it still has that sticky, heavy sweaty feel to it. He walks past his boss Sally Clamp's office. "Hi Sally. Sorry I'm late. There were tons of traffic." He's too proud to admit the real reason.

"Are you all right? You look pale. And your shirt's all rumpled."

"The air conditioning in the car picked this morning to die on me. It got kind of hot in the car sitting in all that traffic."

"Oh. You really don't look well. Why don't you get something to eat."

Bill resists the urge to explode at the third person who has told him to eat breakfast this morning. "I'm fine, really."

"If you say so. Did you have a good holiday weekend?"

"It was fine." Bill would ask Sally about her weekend, but he really doesn't care.

"Good, lets hope it can set you on the right track, and you can get back to being the old Bill Press, the best seller at Prevail Marketing." Sally smiles.

"Let's hope so." Bill walks out into the cold room towards his station. It's the first air conditioning he has felt all day. He sees Sarah and smiles at her. She smiles back. The cold air fills his lungs. His chest tightens.

Breathing becomes difficult. Oddly, though, it feels good.

Bill settles into his chair, and puts his headset on for a day of talking on the telephone. He looks at his list for his first victim. Down in the dark, damp basement of his building is this elaborate computer set-up, that puts together the lists for the salespeople to call. Those geeky computer operators input all of this crap, and out pops the list. But they are nothing if the salespeople cannot sell the products. Today, Bill is selling those beeper systems for old people who fall and can't get up. It's a pager they wear around their necks, and when these old widows are home by themselves, and something happens to them, they can press the beeper, and the entire police and ambulance departments come to their door, or so the sales pitch says. So today, Bill's list is filled with the names of ancient people, so old they fart dust. The list is topped by a Mrs. Esther Nussbaum. Bill dials her number. He's ready to start talking very loudly, for surely Mrs. Nussbaum's hearing is failing, but the number just rings and rings and rings. Maybe she's already dead, Bill thinks. Next on the non-alphabetized list is Mrs. Phyllis Howell. Why don't they alphabetize these lists? Millions of dollars in computer equipment, those geeks with the pocket organizers working them, and they can't even alphabetize a list. It would make it a lot easier for Bill to keep order if they were alphabetized. Mrs. Howell's number rings and rings and rings, too, with no answer. Haven't these old women heard of answering machines? Bill puts his headset down. Old people. They smell, they walk slow, they talk slow, they can't hear a word you say. And they are always alone. Bill hates old people.

More than that, Bill hates a day where he can't reach anyone on the phone. And this is one such day. Maybe all of these people are out at their doctors or having cataract surgery or something. But whatever it is, he hasn't spoken to anyone all morning. On one hand, he's relieved: he doesn't have to talk to old people. But on the other hand, he's not making any money, and not talking to anyone for the entire morning has Bill feeling badly. Good thing lunch is coming, and Sarah. But just then he sees Sarah, heading for the door. "Where are you going?"

"I have a date for lunch," she answers with a coy smile. Before Bill can say "but," she's out the door. Bill just sits there stunned. How dare she have a lunch date? They always eat lunch together. They have the unspoken bond. Bill really doesn't care who she's having lunch with, all he knows it's not him. And now what the hell is he supposed to do for lunch? He can do like he does when Sarah's out sick, he can just work through lunch. But he can't get anyone on the phone, and he's famished, what with passing out and all. He'd take his lunch back to his desk, but then he'd get food all over the place, and have to smell it all day. How dare she? And why today, when he can finally tell her he's a free man, that they can now do all of the things they've been thinking about, that is, if Sarah's been thinking about them too.

The waiter shows Bill to one of those small tables on the far wall of the restaurant, after the waiter had to make a point of saying "Just one for runch?" in his Chinese accent. Bill sits down, and looks around at all of the other tables. There's a table of five people, obviously people who work together, sitting around laughing. There are several couples scattered about. Bill can't tell if they are actually couples, or just people who have that unspoken lunch date everyday like he thought he and Sarah had. Of course, on this day, he's the only person sitting alone. He looks at his menu, as if he's going to order something different than he always orders in this Chinese restaurant: an order of fried dumplings, and sesame chicken. To hell with the cholesterol count. If Bill has to eat alone, he might as well eat good food. He puts his menu down, but quickly picks it back up again because he doesn't know what else to do. He wishes he had brought a newspaper or something to read. That would give him something to do except look around and look stupid. It's times like this Bill wishes he smoked. Someone sitting alone smoking looks a lot better than someone sitting alone staring into space. Suddenly, Bill looks up, because he's sure someone is looking at him. But of course, no one is. Bill always looks at people eating alone, so naturally, he assumes people are looking at him. Luckily, the waiter comes, and placing his order gives him five seconds to be with someone else. After doing that, Bill asks the waiter a question so he won't leave. But the waiter doesn't understand English, only orders, so he just smiles, nods his head like people do when they don't understand a word you just said, and walks away. Bill runs his fingers through his hair, cleans his sunglasses with his tie, opens his wallet and counts his money, and takes his watch off and puts it back on several times, just to keep himself occupied, all the while looking around, to make sure no one is looking at him. Where can Sarah be? And then as an afterthought, Where can Helen be? He hasn't thought much about his wife since he she left on Sunday. She called yesterday, to see how his mother in law was doing, but other than that, he hasn't spoken to her. He wonders if she's alone, and he wonders what exactly is going through her mind. And he wonders why he cares enough to wonder, but not enough to do anything about it.

Another solo diner walks into the restaurant. It's a woman, a pretty woman, someone who shouldn't be eating alone, someone who should never be alone. But there she is, being led to the table in front of Bill's, all by herself. She is seated facing him. He looks at her. She takes off her sunglasses, primps her hair, and gives her order to the waiter. No pretense of looking at the menu like Bill did. Bill wants to watch her every move, but there are none. She just sits there, confidently, waiting for her food to arrive. She doesn't pretend to keep busy, she doesn't look around the restaurant, and she's not concerned about people looking at her. She knows the secret. She has that power. Bill would give anything to ask her what that power is, but he can't. Bill is mesmerized by her, by the ease in which she's able to be alone. Bill is at once impressed and disgusted by her. He wishes she'd just leave, but he also hopes she stays, not in the least because with her around, he's not the only one alone. But she really isn't alone, is she?

Bill walks back into the office. He's sweating from walking so fast. Beads of sweat are dripping from his temples. He walks past Sally Clamp's office without stopping. "Where's your other half?" Bill hears as he walks by. Bill backtracks. "Excuse me?"

"Where's Sarah? Every day at this time, I see you two coming back from lunch. Did she stand you up today?" Sally has a distinctive attitude in her voice. But what it is exactly escapes Bill.

"No, she didn't stand me up," Bill answers defensively. "She had other plans. It's not like we're married or anything. We just go to lunch together sometimes."

"Sometimes?! How about all the time."

"Anyway…" Bill really doesn't want to have this conversation, especially since Sally has a bug up her ass about it.

"So who did you go to lunch with?" Sally just won't let up.

"I went by myself."

"You didn't have to do that. I would have gone with you."

"You always eat lunch in. I thought you couldn't leave the office."

"Sure I can."

"I didn't know that."

"Of course not, you never asked."

Bill pauses. "Well, I've got to get back to work," he finally says.

"Of course," is Sally's response.

Sarah comes waltzing back in from lunch about five minutes late. She whisks over to Bill's area and stops. "How was your lunch?" she asks him with that damn smile on her face, as if she doesn't know she forced him to be alone.

"My lunch was fine. But I wasn't the one with the lunch date. How was your little lunch?" a slightly bitter Bill asks. She just gives him that sly smile, says, "See you later," and prances away. Bitch. Why does he like her so much?

-14-

Helen's in the kitchen, fixing dinner. Jerry likes dinner promptly at 6:00, as Helen found out the night before. Jerry went into a rage to find out Helen spent her day off Monday watching soap operas and not cooking dinner. Jerry said "Dinner at six, every night." Helen thought Jerry was going to slap her, but Jerry didn't. Jerry really isn't a bad person. Jerry just likes things the way Jerry likes them. So if Helen has to make sure dinner is ready at 6:00, what's the big deal? Helen can't stop thinking about Bill. For six years, she cooked for Bill, now she's cooking for someone else. It's weird. But then again, this whole thing is very strange. Bill, living with Helen's mother. And Helen, living with Jerry. Helen hears the door open and slam shut. Jerry's home. This makes her both happy and nervous. The newness of this relationship is exciting, but Jerry is so unpredictable. You never know what kind of mood Jerry will be in. With Bill, it was always the same. Maybe that's what's so exciting. Jerry walks into the kitchen, looks at the clock and looks at Helen's progress. "Gonna be done by six?"

"Yes. With plenty of time to spare," Helen says quite proudly, her back still to Jerry, washing dishes.

"Good." Jerry approaches Helen from the rear, and grabs her breasts. Helen doesn't like this. She feels like she's being manhandled. But what can she say? That's Jerry. "Do you have time to spare for me?" Jerry whispers in Helen's ear.

"I always have time for you," a genuinely excited Helen answers. Helen turns around, and kisses Jerry on the lips. Jerry's tongue goes deep into Helen's mouth. Jerry lifts Helen's shirt off. She's not wearing a bra. Jerry proceeds to lick Helen's nipples. They instantly turn hard. Jerry lifts Helen onto the kitchen counter, and slips off her sweatpants. Jerry spreads Helen's legs, and plunges two fingers into Helen's already moist vagina. Helen lets out a gasp. It hurts. Jerry is being a little rough. But oh, how it hurts so good. Helen leans back. Her back is now up against the cabinet. Jerry begins to suck Helen's clitoris. Jerry bites it. Helen lets out a scream. Whether it's pain or ecstasy, Helen's doesn't even know. Jerry doesn't seem to care. When Jerry's done, Helen stands up. She begins to take Jerry's shirt off, but Jerry knocks Helen's hands away. Jerry is in one of those moods again. So Helen just lies down on the floor, and looks up as Jerry's pants come off. Helen spreads her legs, and Jerry mounts her. Their bodies touch. Jerry's rough shirt feels good on Helen's breasts. And further down, they rub together, two parts meshing as if they were made for each other. Jerry lets out a groan, suddenly stops, and gets up. "I'll get ready for dinner." Helen is left naked, lying on the kitchen floor. She stays there for a moment, thinking. She's never been so turned on in her life.

-15-

His mother in law is in the kitchen, fixing dinner. What culinary delights await him tonight? Maybe some hard pasta. Or some inedible well done steak, like last night. Bill figures he'll be nice to her tonight, so he walks into the kitchen. "Hi."

She turns around. "You looka tired."

"I'm fine, and how are you?," he says sarcastically.

"How comea you looka like that."

"How come I look like what?"

"Like that."

"Because this is the way I look, all right."

"Probably because you don'ta eat breakfast." Bill just shakes his head and goes upstairs. The house is hot. And in every room, a cloud of cigarette smoke hangs in the air, even in his own bedroom. What possible reason would she have to be in his bedroom? She can only make the bed once a day. He checks his cash in the jewelry box, just to make sure she didn't steal anything. She didn't. Bill takes off his work clothes, and slips into a pair of shorts and a tank top. But still, he's hot. And why not? It's 90 degrees, and the air conditioner is off. Bill closes all of the windows upstairs, and when he gets to the bottom of the stairs, flicks on the central air conditioning. The noise brings his mother in law out of the kitchen. "You shouldn'ta turn ona the air condition."

"And why not?"

"Because you beinga hot, the air condition will makea you sick."

"Yeah, sure," he says smugly, as he closes the last of windows. Yep, the air conditioning is on. Bill got his way. He stands there proudly in the middle of the living room, his arms arrogantly folded on his chest, as his mother in law retreats to the kitchen. She mutters something under her breath, but Bill doesn't care what it is. He won his battle. Next, the war.

After turning on all the lights again, and negotiating his way around the damn coffee table, Bill joins his mother in law in the living room. She's sitting there on the couch, a blanket wrapped around her, a cigarette hanging out of her mouth. What man wouldn't want her? Dinner wasn't too bad, actually. Pot roast that was all right, if not sliced a little too thick. She didn't talk much through dinner, except to say how cold it was in the house. Bill looks at her. Actually, she's not such a bad looking woman, as far as older women go. She's not fat, and her Italian mustache is not too thick, although she's sure to grow more facial hair once menopause sets in, but that's not for a few more years. If she wasn't so irritating to be around, Bill is sure she could meet some guy and get married, and leave Bill alone. But that won't happen. Once he and Helen get back together, they'll be stuck with her until she drops dead from lung cancer, which probably isn't too far off, either, what with all the cigarettes she smokes. But what if Helen never comes back? Just then, his mother in law asks "Did you speaka to Helen today?"

What is she, a mind reader? "No."

"Why not?"

"Because she didn't call me."

"Why didn't you calla her?"

"Because I don't know where she is."

"Why didn't you calla her at work?"

Good question. "Because I was busy on the phone all day at work, trying to sell stuff."

"You couldn'ta find a minute to call her. I'ma sure you weren'-ta busy all day." Is she taping his calls, too, Bill wonders. He doesn't answer. "Why dida she leave?"

"I don't know, I've already told you."

"You musta donea something to make her leave."

"What makes you think I did something." The idea infuriates him. "I didn't do anything. Ask her. She'll tell you. It's all her fault."

"You wanna know what I think?" Bill hopes his silence will be taken as a no, but of course, it isn't. "I thinka you don'ta love her anymore."

Bill's interest is peaked. "Really. What makes you say that?" For the first time in his relationship with his mother in law, Bill actually wants to hear what she has to say.

"It's just the feeling I get."

"That's it?" Bill is genuinely disappointed.

"Yeah. I justa don't think you werea making her happy any-more, because you don'ta love her."

Bill thinks about it for a moment. It's a curious idea. But look who it's coming from. Some stupid women wrapped in a blanket in the middle of the summer. Some chain smoking immigrant. A woman who uses store-brand vinegar, not even Heinz, for crying out loud, to wash her private parts. She's the type of person who makes assumptions on other people's lives based on her own experiences. At some point, her dead husband probably stopped loving her, and who could blame him, so now she thinks just because it happened to her, it's happening to everyone else. She has all the answers. She's never wrong. Well, this time she is.

"You're wrong." Bill gets up smacks his leg against the damn coffee table, and heads upstairs. Before he begins climbing the stairs,
though, he turns up the air conditioner, to send more shivers up
and down his mother in law's spine. It's only fair, since she's doing
the same thing to him.

How crazy is that woman?, Bill thinks, as he flips on the base- ·
ball game. He lies down on his bed, feeling a little weak and out
of breath from climbing up the stairs. He's felt this way all day.
Must be the heat. Sure he loves Helen. He always had. Well, not
always. He remembers the first time he laid eyes on her. All
through the years, he's surprised he remembers. It was not a mon-
umentous occasion in his life. There he was, 19 year old, the new
guy at the supermarket, and he was going to lunch with the guy
training him. Just as they were about to walk out the door, a voice
from behind asked, "Howie, where are you going?" Howie and
Bill turned around, and there was Helen. Bill looked at her. Tall,
thin, dark hair, dark eyes, very pretty. But nothing to go nuts over.
She was the kind of girl who just turned pretty. Being tall and
thin, she was probably gawky in high school, the type no one
asked out on a date. It looked to Bill like she had just come into
her own in the past couple of years. "Going to lunch," Howie
answered. "Wait, maybe we'll go with you." And Helen ran off.
Howie said "Forget it, let's go." Bill wanted to say, Hey, wait
for the chicks.
But he didn't, because he was afraid Howie would leave, and
he'd have to eat lunch alone. So they walked out, leaving Helen
behind. Bill asked about her at lunch. "She's like a sister to me."
A sister, huh? "Yeah, she's got a boyfriend." Oh, and that was the
end of that. Bill was not all that disappointed Helen had a
boyfriend. By the time lunch was over, he had pretty much forgotten all about her.

Bill still hasn't caught his breath, so he breathes in deep. The cool air fills his nostrils, then down to his chest, allowing him to feel the air going down. It's as if he can close his eyes, and visualize the air, closing up his lungs, trying to take the life out of him.

But if he closes his eyes, he can't watch the ballgame. The Mets are down. There's a guy on the mound Bill has never heard of. When Bill was younger, he knew every player, every transaction, knew how many R.B.I.s each player had. But as he got older, he lost track. The players changed. He never really lost interest, but with other things on his mind, he just couldn't follow them as closely. With the weight of the world on his shoulders, the Mets, the love of his life when he was younger, must now take a back seat. It's kind of a passing fancy now. If he has time, he'll watch a game. If not, oh well, what are you going to do? He's sure the Mets would understand.

Bill hears his mother in law downstairs. She's changing channels, talking Italian on the phone—his phone, and his phone bill. She's probably talking long distance to some shack in Sicily that just got a phone last week. Or maybe she's talking to Helen.

Bill looks around the bedroom. There's his side of the bed, with all his stuff. Helen's side is empty. It's just not fair. And Helen isn't even here anymore. Bill gets up, his head still a little woozy. He feels a little cold, but he refuses to lower the air conditioner. Let her suffer. He lifts up his weights. They feel heavier than ever. He walks on the bed, and drops them on the floor, on Helen side of the bed. "Hey, what area you doing upa there?" Shut up and mind your own damn business. But instead, Bill says "Nothing." Then he lifts the bench and deposits it next to the weights. Now, at least, he'll be able to pass on his side of the bed. Feeling even more weak, Bill moves the television back into the corner. Then he wheels his desk chair through the space between the bed and the dresser, and out the door into the hallway. Next, standing on his side of the bed, he takes hold of his queen-sized mattress by those little handles they give you, and pulls the mattress off the box spring. He stands it up, but he just can't hold it. It folds over on him, pinning him against his desk. He's able to push it up, and drag it out the door. He's sweating profusely. And he's cold. But he pushes on. The box spring is next, easier because it's solid. Then he disassembles the frame, and stands it against the wall in the hall. Luckily, the desk is on wheels, so he pushes it through the vacated space where the bed was, and over to Helen's side of the room. He stops to clear away the weights and the bench. The sweat drips off him as he bends over. Bill gives the desk one last push, and it's against the wall. Well, it's not actually against the wall. It's against Helen's closet. But that's okay. She doesn't live here anymore. Then he pushes the weights and the bench against the desk. "What'sa going on upa there?" Bill sits on the floor. He doesn't feel well. He'd like to lie down, but his bed is in the hallway. He can't stop now. So he drags himself up, and tries to assemble the frame. But he can't get the two pieces together, for his vision is blurred, and he sees colors before his eyes, therefore making it difficult. Somehow, though, he connects the pieces, and the frame is together. He takes his shirt off, and goes for the box spring. He drops it on the frame. Now, the mattress. He tries to push it into the bedroom, but it just bends. So he pulls, sapping most of the energy he has left. He's backing it in, when he trips on the box spring, and falls on top of it. The mattress lands on him. He tries to push it off, but he simply does not have the strength. He's suffocating. Bill will die underneath this mattress, he thinks. What a freaky way to die. Bill always thought drowning would be the worst way to go, but this has changed his mind. Getting trapped under a mattress so you can rearrange your bedroom while your mother in law sits downstairs smoking and talking Italian possibly to your estranged wife is the worst way to die. He just wishes he can tell someone, but he can't, because he's dead. He can call for help, but help would mean his mother in law. No thanks. Bill wonders if he really does still love Helen. It's moot now, now that he's dead, but he wonders if he does. He guesses he'll never know. Bill suddenly feels better. Maybe laying down for a few minutes with little air is what he needed. So just like Bill Bixby/Lou Ferrigno, he's able to lift the mattress off of him, and escape certain death. Bill gets the mattress on the box spring, and collapses. But something is bothering him. His chair is still in the hall. It belongs at his desk. He considers leaving it there, what with just facing death's door and all, but he just can't. So he gets up, and wheels the chair in, using it like a walker, like an old person. To get the chair to it's proper place, he must first move his weights, his bench, push the chair in, and move everything back. With this done, he can relax, everything is in its proper place. He lies back down on the bed, the bed that nearly killed him, the bed where Bill and Helen had spent their wedding night. But the Mets game is on, and his television is off. Bill can get up to move his chair, that was important. But he just can't seem to gather up the energy for the Mets. He just doesn't care anymore.

-16-

Helen walks into the bedroom. Bill sits up. Behind Helen there is a person. Bill can't make out the face. But it's not really a person. It's more of a presence. A frightening presence. Helen doesn't say a word. The sight of Helen and this thing scares Bill. He pulls the cover up around his neck, hoping it will protect him. Helen walks to the foot of the bed. She strips off all of her clothing, and gets into bed with Bill. Bill remains under the covers, shivering. But Helen doesn't get into the bed alone. That presence tucks itself in as well. Helen moves to Bill's side of the bed, and kisses him. Bill closes his eyes, but he can still see the presence, looking at him, laughing at him. Bill opens his eyes, and it's his mother in law who's in bed with him. But the presence is gone. Bill jumps out of the bed. His mother in law is laughing. "I knew it alla alonga."

Bill wakes up, sweating, shaking, near tears. His pillow and cover are drenched with sweat. His immediate thought is his idiot mother in law turned off the air conditioning, but no, it's still on. Bill is still shivering, but he's not sure if it's from fright or illness. His walking quite unsteady, Bill makes it to the bathroom and gets the thermometer, but not before dropping a bottle of Tylenol and the Pepto-Bismol in the sink. He gets back into bed to wait the required three minutes to find out what's wrong with him. While he's laying there, his mother in law steps into his room. She must have heard him thrashing about the bathroom, but having just had that dream, Bill pulls the cover tightly around his neck. He's not taking any chances. "Whatsa matter?"

"Nuttin," is all Bill can spit out.

She flips on the light, blinding Bill. "Why area you taking youra temperature."

Bill takes the thing out of his mouth. "No reason." Even illness cannot take away his sarcasm. Bill wishes she'd leave his bedroom, but instead she ventures in further.

"Let me feela youra head." But just as she's about to touch Bill's forehead, he remembers his dream. "Just get out of here, please," and he knocks her hand away. "Alla right." And out she goes. Bill puts the thermometer back in his mouth. He feels a little bad about yelling at his mother in law. But he had no choice, really. Bill then begins to feel a lot bad when he looks at the thermometer: 103 degrees. Bill's sick. There will be no going to work in the morning. No telling Sarah he's a free man. No, he'll spend the day in bed, with his mother in law in the house. He can't think of anything worse.

"Hi Sally, it's Bill. I can't come in today. I'm sick," Bill tells his boss Sally Clamp over the phone.

"Really? You seemed fine yesterday."

Bill immediately gets defensive. "You think I'm faking it," he says angrily.

"No, Bill, relax. I'm just concerned. And please don't talk to me like that."

That's right, Bill thinks, a boss should be treated with more respect than that. "I'm sorry. I just thought you were accusing me of something. You're right, I shouldn't talk to my boss that way."

"Hmm" is all Sally Clamp can muster.

Bill continues, oblivious to the response. "I felt lousy last night. I then I woke up in the middle of the night with a fever."

"All right. If there's anything I can do, please call me."

"I'm okay."

"That's right, you have your wife there to take care of you."

"Hmm" is all Bill Press can muster.

Sally continues, fully aware of the response. "You better come back soon. Sarah needs her lunch partner back," with a definite hint of sarcasm, which goes completely over Bill's head.

"See you tomorrow, hopefully."

"Again, don't hesitate to call."

"Yeah, yeah, bye," and Bill hangs up the phone. It's cold in the bedroom. The one day his stupid mother in law decides to leave the air conditioner on, he's sick. And where is she, anyway? He hasn't heard a peep out of her. It's past the time he usually leaves for work, and she hasn't even come in to see if he's all right. He could be dead for all she knows. Real nice mother in law. Bill doesn't stop to think about his treatment of his real nice mother in law the night before, or since he didn't hear a peep out of her, maybe she could be dead for all he knows. Nice son in law. So Bill gets out of bed, and goes downstairs. And there's his mother in law, sitting in a cloud of smoke on the living room couch, sipping coffee, fully dressed. She doesn't look up. So Bill says "I'm sick. I'm not going to work." She just looks at him. She says nothing. "Don't you want to know what's wrong with me?"

"What'sa wrong witha you?," she asks robotically.

"I don't know. I have a fever." Still nothing. "I guess I should have some tea, huh? My mother always said you should have tea when you're sick." Nothing. Bill can't figure out what's wrong with her. "Well, I guess I'll make myself some tea. I'm going into the kitchen right now."

"Good fora you." More sarcasm lost on Bill. He makes his little tea, and sits down in his chair, but not before negotiating around the coffee table. Bill thinks he's getting really good at this. He's just about to say something relatively pleasant to his mother in law, when she gets up. "Where are you going?"

"Out."

"Out where?"

"Out."

"Why?"

"Because it'sa the summer. And I want to be out." And out she goes. So now Bill is left drinking tea, sitting in his cold house, sick. And now, he's alone. Bill can only shake his head in wonderment. They're always around, unless you need them, and then they leave.

"Hello, is Helen Press there please?"

"Who's calling," the snotty woman asks on the other end.

"Her husband." Bill is put on hold without even a 'hold on' or 'one moment.' Bitchy group of women work in that office. It's probably at the root of all of Helen's problems.

"Hi, Bill." Helen sounds both happy to hear from Bill, yet annoyed at the intrusion.

"Hi."

"What's going on?"

"Nothing, what about you?"

"Nothing. How's it going?"

"Fine."

"That's not what I heard," Helen answers cryptically.

"What have you heard? And from whom?"

"My mother met me here for lunch." So that's where she went. "She says you're sick."

"Yeah, I woke up-"

"Yeah, she told me you woke up. And she told me what you did."

"What did I do?"

"Oh, come on Bill. Don't deny it. Mom told me all about it. How could you, Bill? I know you don't like her, but still, to do that, to hit her."

Hit her? "Hit her?!"

"Yeah, she was just trying to help."

Oh yeah, he pushed her hand away when she tried to feel his head. But what else could he do, under the circumstances? He changes the subject. "So how are you doing?"

"Fine."

"So you ready to tell me who you are living with?"

"No. And I'm not ready to drop the subject of you hitting my mother."

"Yeah, yeah, yeah." Bill is growing bored of his mother in law, and, come to think of it, with Helen.

"Fuck you too," and Helen ends the conversation.

Bill sits in his chair, the phone still in his hand, listening to the dial tone. It's the only sound in the house. A solitary figure, listening to a dial tone. Bill really did want to talk to Helen. He wanted to talk to anyone, so he would feel like someone was there in the house with him. Bill can't remember the last time he was alone in this house. He always left for work before Helen. He always came home after her. If Bill put down the phone, the house would become silent. The silence scares Bill. Because the silence says a lot. Bill knows that. But he just can't figure out just what the silence is telling him. God, he wants Helen back. At this point, he'd even settle for her mother.

-17-

"I trust you're feeling better after your long weekend?" a cheery Sally Clamp says to Bill as he tries to sneak past her office Monday morning.

"Yeah, I'm fine. The fever didn't break until Friday afternoon." Bill was happy for the time off from work. Maybe a few days off is what he'll need to become the old Bill Press, the best seller at Prevail Marketing. On the other hand, being home with the Disagreeable Widow was no bargain. After apologizing for smacking her hand away ("it must have been fever-induced delirium"), his mother in law acted like the prototypical mother, taking care of Bill at his bedside. Although, every time, while she was vertical as Bill lay horizontally under her, he was wary of the situation.

"Well, we missed you around here."

"I missed you guys," a lie, almost. And where is Sarah, anyway? Bill hasn't stopped thinking about her since he got sick. And he hasn't stopped now. He looks around for her, as Sally goes on about some nonsense.

"Bill, are you listening to me, or are you looking for something, or someone?"

"No, no, no. I'm listening." He spots Sarah. "See you later." Sally is left standing there, as she watches the two lunch partners reunite.

"Hi Sarah."

"Hey Bill."

Bill waits. But she says nothing. "So, I'm back."

"Were you out?"

She must be joking. "Yeah, I've been out since Wednesday."

"Oh," she says with that sly smile.

This time, Bill takes the initiative. "I'll tell you all about my illness at lunch."

"Can't."

Can't?! Bill's been waiting more than a week to tell her he's a free man, and she says can't?! "Why not?"

"I'm having lunch with Sally. She asked me."

"Is this a business thing?"

"No, she said she wants to get to know me better." And Sarah walks off confidently, if not arrogantly.

Bill wonders why Sally would want to get to know Sarah better. There's not much substance to her, really. Sarah would do well to take some lessons from Sally. A successful, self-made, business-woman. Sally is a fine woman. Why would she want to know Sarah?

Bill steps out into the balmy July heat. 92 degrees, with humidity to match. Weather like this makes the back of Bill's hair curl up. He hates that. He has decided to take a walk. He doesn't feel like sitting at his desk, and he wasn't invited to the little women's luncheon. Bill can't believe he's been a bachelor for more than a week, and he hasn't even told Sarah yet. Hell, he can't believe he's a bachelor at all.

He walks along the street, looking at all the people passing by. He'll grab a hot dog later. There are those young would-be businessmen, carrying the attache case their parents bought them as a graduate present from business school, wearing their $100 suits, thinking they look like Armanis. There are the blue collar workers sitting on the fountains, eating the tuna fish sandwiches their ugly housewives packed for them, plotting their next infidelity.

There are women, lots of them, short ones, fats ones, pretty ones, tall ones, all walking in pairs or threes or more, all smiling and laughing and giggling, none of them looking at Bill. His hair must be curling up really badly.

It's hot. The sweat is dripping down Bill's brow. He stops for a hot dog and a Pepsi, sits down on a bench, and eats. At the bench across from him is this couple. They are both big and fat. Really big, really fat. The guy must weigh about 300 pounds, his lovely bride 250. They are sitting there eating lunch. Hamburgers, hot dogs, knishes, chicken legs, potato chips, etc. etc. etc. Glandular problem my ass. They are the typical happy-go-lucky, jolly fat people. They are talking with everyone who stops by, making comments about how hot it is.

Seems they just got married, and are enjoying their honeymoon right here in the sweltering city. They both have "I Love New York" t-shirts on, and on the back they put "And each other." How cute. Bill looks at them with pity. They are two disgusting human beings. Everyone who walks by them must be laughing at them, these two pathetic losers, sitting on a park bench, eating lunch. Bill certainly does pity them. Little do they know.

When they think no one is looking, they gaze into each other's eyes, and mouth the words "I love you." And then they kiss, their big fat sweaty faces joined as one. Bill wants to barf up the lunch he just scarfed down. Bill can't take it any more. He gets up and leaves, but takes one last look back at this gruesome twosome. They do look happy, though.

Bill gets back from his "lunch" break. He walks by Sally's office. She's back from her little lunch meeting with Sarah. Why did Sally do it? She's probably jealous Bill and Sarah go to lunch together, so she just wanted to get Sarah away from him. He stops into her office. "Hi, Sally. How was your lunch?"

She looks at him a moment. She smiles. "Fine." And with that, she turns away. It's obvious she doesn't want to speak any further with Bill. It's odd. Bill is always trying to get out of her office, but Sally usually just rambles on. Oh well, Bill leaves, and sees Sarah from across the room.

"How was your lunch?"

"Fine." And Sarah turns and walks away. Odd, these women.

-18-

Helen was working late. That's when it happened. It was only her and Jerry in the office. Helen was a little nervous about it, what with those comments Jerry was always making to her. But she was a married woman, certainly Jerry knew that. Jerry would never try anything. The memory still stirs Helen. If she could choose to have only one memory, this would be the one, the first time with Jerry.

Helen was at her desk. Jerry was nearby, also working late, or pretending to. Helen never really was attracted to Jerry. Just not her type at all. But Helen looked at Jerry, and she started to think about it. Jerry was not particularly good looking. But what was she thinking about? She's married. She could never do that to Bill. Or Jerry, for that matter.

But then Jerry walked over, saying here they were, all alone in the office, the first time they've been alone since that time in the supply room, when Jerry kissed Helen, and Helen ran out sobbing. Later, Helen didn't know why she was crying. Was it because Jerry kissed her, or was it because she wanted Jerry to kiss her. Or maybe it was because she wanted someone, anyone, to kiss her. Hell, Bill certainly wasn't doing it. Bill hadn't touched her for months, but she didn't know if it was Bill's doing, or her's. She really didn't want to be with Bill, and it appeared Bill didn't particularly want to be with her. It always seemed he had something else on his mind. But then again, so did Helen.

Helen remained sitting down, working, as Jerry hovered over her. Jerry just stood there, staring at Helen. Helen couldn't concentrate on her work. She knew what Jerry was thinking, and she wasn't sure if she was thinking the same thing. But this was it, she knew it. It was now or never. Her whole relationship with Bill passed before her eyes. He was once so loving, so caring, so attentive. Now, it was all different. And she was not sure if it was Bill who changed, or her. She wasn't sure of anything anymore. Bill used to look at her with such desire in his eyes. But now, he doesn't. Helen looked up at Jerry. And now Jerry had that look. Helen didn't know what to do. What happened to her marriage? At that instant, she decided it really didn't matter. She pressed her lips against Jerry's. Jerry's tongue went right down her throat. It felt so good. Helen stood up while they kissed. Jerry towered over her. Jerry grabbed Helen's breasts. Helen's ran her hands over Jerry's chest. It was so much different than Bill's. Jerry cleared everything off of Helen's desk. This act of power, of violence even, turned Helen on. Jerry began to rip off Helen's clothing. Helen did the same to Jerry, and they were both naked. Helen stopped for a moment, and looked at Jerry's body. Jerry looked different just standing there nude, exposed. She thought of Bill. A tear came to her eye. But it didn't have a chance to fall, because Jerry lifted Helen onto the desk, and laid her down. Jerry immediately started licking Helen's clitoris. It felt amazingly good. Bill could never do it like that. Jerry's tongue licked it ever so lightly, then harder, to the point where it almost hurt. Then Jerry's tongue was deep inside her. At the same time, Jerry's finger slipped into Helen's ass. Bill had never done that. Helen had never thought of having anyone do it, but with Jerry forcing a finger in there, it felt so good.

Suddenly, Jerry stopped, and looked at Helen. Jerry's eyes said 'your turn,' and Jerry laid down on the desk. Oral sex was never one of her favorites. Bill used to try to force her head down there, but Helen would refuse. But with Jerry laying there, hips gyrating, Helen couldn't resist. Slowly, tentatively, Helen stuck her tongue out of her mouth, and licked Jerry. It tasted surprisingly good. Helen licked again. Jerry's back arched. Helen began to smile. For the first time in her life, she liked being between someone's legs. Helen began to lick and suck, and Jerry was screaming in pleasure. Just as Jerry was about to come, Jerry told her to stop. It was time. Jerry got up. Helen laid down on the desk, and spread her legs. Jerry got on top. When their genitals touched, a warm feeling came over Helen. Her clitoris was rubbing against Jerry as Jerry pushed and pushed. Jerry was going wild. Bill never went crazy like this. He always had to stop, or else he'd come. But Jerry never stopped. Helen had never felt this way before.

It started slowly. Helen felt it in her clitoris, then in her vagina. Jerry continued to pound away, Helen's clitoris rubbing against Jerry. The pressure started building and building inside of Helen. She closed her eyes, and gripped her nails into Jerry's back. Then at once, the pressure was released. As she was coming, Helen knew right then and there her marriage was over.

Jerry came soon thereafter. Quickly, Jerry was up, getting dressed. But Helen simply laid there on her desk, naked, her legs spread wide open. She stared at Jerry walking around the room. God, she thought, who ever thought it would feel like that with a woman.

-19-

.

"I saw Helen today," Bill's mother in law says suddenly during dinner.

Bill looks up just as suddenly, then composes himself. "Oh, really," he says disinterested.

"Yeah. I saw her ata work."

"How is she?"

"What do youa care? You never calla her. All of a sudden you wanta know how she is?"

"So don't tell me if you don't want to. I don't care."

"She'sa fine."

"Good for her."

After a moment he asks, "Do you know where she's staying?"

"She wouldn'ta tella me. She justa said she's staying with a friend froma work."

"A woman?"

"Yeah, that'sa what she said."

"Good."

"It'sa strange. She looksa happy sometime, then other times she looksa sad. I thinka she's confused."

"Me too," Bill says, as he throws his napkin into his plate, signaling the end of dinner.

"I thinka if you called her, and asked her to come back, she'da come."

"Well, I'm not about to do that. I'll let her figure this out on her own. If she wants to come back, she can. And if she doesn't..." Bill lets that hang in the air. What if she doesn't come back? Bill has never really thought about it. For these past two weeks, he has just assumed she would come back. But what if she doesn't?

Over the course of their marriage, there were times when Helen would come home late, or not call when she was supposed to. In those rare times that Bill was alone in the house, these horrible thoughts would run through his head, that she was lying on the side of the road, dead. Or she'd been abducted by some lunatic. The mental health profession calls these thoughts "intrusions," horrible thoughts that pop into a person's mind, but something they don't in their wildest imagination want to come true. At these times, Bill would think how terrible it would be if Helen died, how they wouldn't spend the rest of their lives together and grow old. Now Helen's gone, maybe for good. And as far as Bill is concerned, it's just as if she is dead. But oddly enough, it doesn't seem so bad. Maybe they weren't intrusions after all.

"So what area you going toa do?"

Bill thinks for a moment. What is he going to do? Thoughts of Sarah's blue eyes flash through his head. He smiles and turns on the baseball game. Since Helen left, his appetite for the Mets is back. Sure, the players are different than when he was a big fan years ago, but it's still the Mets, isn't it?

-20-

Jerry sits down at the table. Helen walks over and serves her dinner. They sit silently, eating. Helen looks at Jerry, choking down her food. What is she doing? Why is she living with this woman, cooking for her, cleaning for her, making love with her? Helen is no lesbian. She likes men. She likes having a big hard object inside of her.

"Where's the salt?" So Helen gets up and gets Jerry the salt. The thought of being with a woman makes Helen ill. But for some reason, she does it. And she enjoys it to a certain extent. Helen closes her eyes, and pretends it's a man licking her clitoris, a man's fingers inside her, and man's tongue in her mouth. And when she goes down on Jerry, she just pretends she's masterbating, and licking her fingers and her vibrator after they've been inside her.

Bill hadn't been inside her in months. He'd claim he was too tired. Or he was thinking about work and couldn't get it up. The only time he'd want to do it was when Helen was in a bad mood, or when she had her period. So Helen had to pleasure herself before Bill came home from work. Helen wonders if Bill was doing the same thing. Maybe that's why he always locked the door to the bathroom.

Helen doesn't love Jerry. Jerry does seem to love Helen, though, in her own way. Sure, Jerry yells at her, orders her around, but that's just Jerry's way. Bill was never like that. He was always so passive. "Fine," he'd always say. "Fine." Nothing was ever right, nothing was ever wrong. Everything was just fine.

"I need more soda." So Helen gets up and gets Jerry some soda. Helen still loves Bill. And what's not to love? Bill never made any demands on Helen. She was always free to do whatever she wanted. Sure, Bill was stubborn sometimes. And he had that annoying habit of always cleaning up, always picking up after her. Who could live with someone like that? Everything had to be in its place, or Bill would get angry. And then there was the way Bill would twist Helen's words around, and make her think the way Bill wanted her to think. Helen never even knew what Bill was doing, until she later realized she had changed her mind over to Bill's way of thanking. She hates that about Bill. But he really is kind and sweet.

"I'm done." Jerry leaves the table, and sits on the couch and turns on the T.V. "Hey, the Mets are on." Helen is clearing off the table. Bill is probably watching the Mets game too. She wishes she could be at home, clearing off the dishes, with Bill on their couch, watching the Mets game. She really wants it. But she just can't bring herself to go home. There's something in the way. A presence is there when she's with Bill. And she knows if she goes home, it'll still be there. It was there on the phone last week. Helen knows it won't go away.

They used to be so happy. They were the happiest couple in the world. Everybody looked upon them as the model marriage. After all those years, they still enjoyed each other's company. At parties, while the men and women would break off in separate groups, Bill and Helen would stick together, usually with the other women. Sure, they had minor disagreements, but never anything major.

Bill gave Helen a good, stable life. But then that presence had to come and ruin it all. Why? Why did it have to come? Helen begins to cry softly at the sink. She doesn't want to make any noise, because Jerry will hear her, and know what's she's crying about. And then, Helen will have to lick Jerry's vagina until she comes.

Helen goes back out of the kitchen, to get more dishes. She stops. Jerry does not look up. So Helen blows her nose. "Are you crying?"

"No," Helen answers sheepishly.

"Yes you are. You're thinking of him, aren't you?"

"No."

"Yes you are. You love him, not me."

"No."

"Prove it." So Helen walks over to Jerry, takes her pants down, and proceeds licking. At the same time, Helen puts her hand down her own pants, and slips her finger into her own, already soaking wet vagina.

-21-

She always used to come over to him, and ask him whether or not they'd go to lunch together. It became annoying after a while. Of course they were going to lunch together. But she always asked. Suddenly, though, she doesn't. So now Bill must assume Sarah's role. "Do you want to go to lunch today?"

"Hmm. Lunch." Sarah thinks.

"Yeah, you know, that meal after breakfast," an impatient Bill answers.

"Yeah, sure. I don't have any other plans." She gives that sly smile. He hates her. He really does.

For today's dining experience, this reunion lunch, as it were, this lunch that will change Bill and Sarah's life forever, she picked pizza. "So, it's been a while," Bill says as he wipes off his seat before sitting down on the plastic pizzeria chair.

"What's been a while?"

"That we've been out to lunch."

"Has it?"

He'd love to slap her. She knows it's been a while. "Yeah, a couple of weeks, at least."

"Hmm. I wonder why that is."

"Well, I was sick for a few days, and you had plans a few days..."

"Yeah. Oh well, I guess you got me on an off day today then."

Off day. That's what he's been reduced to. Maybe he shouldn't tell her. Maybe she doesn't like him like that. Maybe he was wrong to assume they had this unspoken thing between them. Maybe it was all in his mind. It must be. She never opens up to him. How much could she like him if she acts like that. She's so cold and aloof. What if he tells her and she laughs at him. His wife has already left him. Bill doesn't think he could take being laughed at by the woman he may be in love with. Bill breaks his trance. "So what have you been up to?"

"Oh, nothing. Working, going out to The Hamptons on the weekends." The Hamptons. Bill and "his wife" were invited out there. Bill waits, but she doesn't mention it. "What have you been up to lately?"

Say it! I've been separated from my wife lately. Say it! It's the opportunity I've been waiting two years for. Be a man! I haven't been able to make love to my wife for months because of you. This is it! For the first time in my life, I'm going to say something on my own, without being forced into it. The timing is perfect. Say it! Bill's chest starts to tighten. The air conditioner must be on. The waiter walks over with the pizza. Bill waited too long.

Sarah picks up a piece of pizza. It's still too hot, so the cheese sticks to the rest of the pie. She's holding it upside down as she brings it over to her plate, so the cheese is dripping all over the table. Bill watches in disgust. How can a person eat like this? Bill waits a few moments for the pizza to cool, so his cheese will not be dripping all over the place. Bill likes a nice, orderly, slice of pizza. But Sarah dives right into the hot pie, halfway done with her first slice before Bill begins eating. She doesn't even consider waiting for Bill. That's not something Sarah does. So Bill must play catch-up, eating fast to even up with Sarah. He eats so fast, he doesn't get to take his sip of Pepsi between bites, thus messing up his pizza-soda ratio.

"So how's your wife?" Sarah says suddenly out of the silence.

Bill is stunned. And his face shows it. "My wife?"

"Yeah, you know, the woman you're married to?"

"I know who she is. Why do you ask?"

"I'm just making conversation."

No she's not. Sarah never just makes conversation. There must be a reason for this line of questioning. And Bill thinks he knows what it is. Sarah wants to know how his relationship with his wife is, to see if she'll ever have a chance with him. The normally closed Sarah has left herself wide open this time. For the first time, Sarah has shown some indication she's interested in Bill. Now, the time is right. "Well, since you ask, my wife moved out a couple of weeks ago."

Sarah sort of smiles. She doesn't say anything. The look in her face shows no shock at this pronouncement that she's Bill's for the asking. She doesn't ask for any details. Bill does not offer any, though he would if she would only ask. "I kind of had a feeling something was going on with you two."

"Oh really, what made you think that?"

"Women just know these things." Sarah is smiling from ear to ear now. So is Bill. The only question he has is, are they smiling at the same thing?

PART III

-22-

The guy filling in for the vacationing newswoman this morning said this has been one of the hottest summers on record. 95 degrees the past two weeks, not to mention the humidity. It's the kind of weather that makes everything stick to you. Walking past a construction site, you can swear the microscopic dirt that you can't even see that has to be falling from it is sticking to your moist skin. And there's nothing you can do to shake it off, short of taking a nice cool shower. Even that doesn't make you feel clean, though, because when you unlock the door and step out of the bathroom, the heat is hanging in the air, and like a magnet, all of the dirt the world generates is drawn to your nice clean skin. It won't end, until the summer ends.

But Bill is cool in his car, the newly repaired air conditioner blowing on his face, going deep into his lungs. But who cares about breathing? It's hot outside. He's driving eastbound, towards Helen's office. Helen figured it was about time they got together. It's been a month since she moved out, and they haven't seen each other since. Bill wanted to meet her yesterday, on a Sunday, at wherever it is she's living. But Helen refused, saying Monday during lunch was better. The drive from Bill's office to Helen's office is an hour and a half, so Bill had to take a half day off from work to go to lunch with his wife. But that's what she wants, so Bill agreed.

What irks Bill the most about this is missing lunch with Sarah. Not that she would go with him. Every day, it's Sarah and Sally, going out to lunch together, giggling when they leave, giggling when the come back. Bill hasn't had a private conversation with Sarah since he told her about Helen. Two weeks that he could have been making love to Sarah are wasted.

The girls, how Bill refers to Sarah and Sally in his mind, asked him to go to lunch with them once. He thought about it, and refused. He would be out of place in this coven of women, talking about whatever it is women talk about. Fabrics, most probably. Bill would be the odd man out, as it were, not understanding the two women, as they talk in their code, talking against men, plotting against them. They'll rule the world some day, these women. Won't that be a frightening thing. Women would finally be free to wield their powers over the universe, the same powers they've been wielding quietly over men, lo these many centuries.

Helen wanted Bill to call her from the lobby, but he decided to go upstairs. He's not quite sure why. He's never been up there, and an office is an office—he's not curious what it looks like, but something is drawing him there. As if that office holds the key.

Bill gets off the elevator at Helen's floor. He takes two steps out, and looks both ways. He doesn't know which way to walk. But he must make a decision soon, because there's a woman barreling down the hall, and Bill is in the way.

"Excuse me," she says nastily, as Bill is still blocking her path, not sure what to do.

"Sorry." They give each other dirty looks as she walks away. Does he know her? No. That must be that dyke Helen told her about months and months ago. Helen said they hired some new woman, and she's just got to be a lesbian. And she must be. About five foot five, fat ass, short hair like a man, no earrings, no make-up. You can't make out her breasts, covered under male clothing. All in all, a lovely, lovely woman.

After vacillating some more, Bill decides to make a decision, and go right. The hallway opens up into one large room, and there's Helen, sitting at her desk. She catches site of him walking towards her, and she gets panicky. What if Jerry sees him? She'll have a fit. But Helen's not sure Jerry even know what Bill looks like. She has no pictures on her desk, and Helen can't recall ever showing Jerry a picture of Bill. "Hi," Bill says as he approaches the desk.

"I thought I told you to call me from downstairs."

"I decided to come up. I was just curious what the place looks like."

"Well, it's an office, just like any other office."

"I see that."

They stand there on opposite sides of the desk, the same desk where Helen and Jerry first had sex. The place where she violently took Helen against her will, and made her come. Seeing Bill standing in the same place Jerry was

standing when she was eating Helen makes her heart sink, but also arouses her. "Let's get out of here," a flustered Helen says after a few moments of silent contemplation. They leave, but they are not alone, for the presence follows them everywhere.

"So how's my mother?" Helen asks, as they sit down at the table. The walk over to the restaurant was silent. Bill wanted to say something, but he couldn't think of anything. Helen had plenty to say, but was waiting for Bill.

"She's fine."

"Are you two getting along?"

"Yeah, for the most part."

"What do you mean, 'for the most part'?" Helen is beginning to get angry.

"Relax. What I mean is, we get along all right, but there are those usual things she does to bug me. Plus, there's the tension of having her live with me, when you're not around."

"Oh, so now you're blaming me. Like it's my fault you two can't get along." She begins to ramble as tears fill her eyes. "Everything is always my fault. But it's not, it's not."

Diners at the other tables look over. "Helen, calm down! I'm not blaming you for anything. Relax, will you please?" Bill waits for Helen to compose herself. "But you've got to admit, it is kind of strange, my mother in law living with me, after my wife has moved out."

"Well, she's got to live somewhere, and she can't live where I'm living." After Helen said this, she realized she shouldn't have. Because this gives Bill the opportunity to open up a whole can of worms she's not ready to talk about right now. But even if she didn't say it, Bill still would have brought it up. He's got a right to know where she's living. But it's none of his business what she's doing.

"So where are you living?"

"I told you, with a friend from work."

"I know. Who?"

"I don't have to tell you."

"Yes you do. I send you money to your work every week, because you say you can't live on your salary. I don't say a word. But I think I have a right to know where and with whom you are living."

"Jerry."

"Jerry?"

"Jerry."

"You're living with a person named Jerry?"

"Yes."

"And this person named Jerry. Would this happen to be a male person, or a female person?"

"It really doesn't make any difference."

"Of course it does, and you know it."

"Female."

"Good." Bill is relieved by this. Helen can only smile. What a naive, simple fool. They sit silently for a moment. Bill is happy Helen's not having an affair with anybody, because that would spell the end of their marriage. So at least now, there's hope. He thinks about making love to Sarah, and knows he has to act quickly, because soon Helen would be coming back to him. Helen, on the other hand, knows she's never coming back. She pretty much confessed her affair, and Bill is oblivious. He really doesn't know her anymore.

The food arrives. Bill ordered a veal parmigiana hero, Helen got the eggplant. Bill goes through the ritual of biting and wiping and sipping, while Helen bites and doesn't wipe, so she gets tomato sauce on her glass. Why does he like these slobs?

"So, have you come to any revelations this past month?" Bill finally asks.

"What do you mean?"

"I mean, have you figured out what's wrong?"

"I think we both know what's wrong."

"I don't."

"That's too bad, then."

"I take it you're not going to tell me."

"It's not the kind of thing I can tell you. You have to figure it out on your own." Somewhere, she can hear the presence laughing. Bill can't hear it, though. He's too busy trying to figure out what's wrong with Helen.

"So are you saying our marriage is over?"

Helen pauses. A warm streak goes over Bill's body, waiting for the answer to a question he never thought he'd have to ask. These things happen to other people, not Bill Press, the best seller at Prevail Marketing. "No," Helen finally answers. "Our marriage is not over." The presence lets out a big guffaw, almost blowing Helen's ear drums out, and bringing her near tears. But the tears go away, because you can't argue with the presence.

-23-

Bill opens the front door, expecting a blast of cool air to hit him in the face. Surely even she must turn on the air conditioner in this unbearable heat. But of course, he's wrong. It's just as hot inside as out. He quickly turns the central air unit on, and goes around the house shutting the windows. The Disagreeable Widow is in the sweltering kitchen, cooking dinner. She's dressed for the heat: shorts, a thin, almost see-through shirt, with no bra. She's bending over the hot oven when Bill walks into the kitchen. The sweat is dripping off her forehead, onto the open over door, where it quickly sizzles away. She stands up, alarmed to see Bill standing there, staring at her. "Whatsa the matter?"

"Nothing," he says, not taking his eyes off her. He never realized how big her breasts are. Then why are Helen's so small? "What's for dinner?"

"Pot roast."

"Good. I'll go change." He goes upstairs, stopping in the bathroom, to wash the day away from him. He locks the door, then reaches into the back of the cabinet, where his secret bar of soap is waiting, waiting to do it's job.

Looking at the soap makes Bill smile. It's his, and only his. It's clean, it can't be touched, not by Helen, or his mother in law, or

Sarah, or Sally Clamp. Bill lathers up his hands, then his face. He cups the water in his hands, and washes his face off, and he watches as the dirty suds go down the drain, gone forever. He dries his precious bar of soap off, puts it back in the paper wrapper, and places it back in his hiding place, where it will be tomorrow, and the day after that, and the day after that, until it's all used up, and then, he'll replace it with a new bar.

In the bedroom, he expects to find his bed made, but it's not. She was not in his room today, her hands didn't touch the place where he sleeps, where he lays his nearly naked body. He takes his shirt and tie and pants off, and hangs them up, replacing them with a t-shirt and jeans. He easily glides through the space between the bed and dresser, and goes downstairs for a meal with his mother in law.

"I saw Helen today," he says as she serves him dinner.

"You did?! Why didn't youa tella me?"

"What do you think I'm doing now?"

"Why didn't youa tella me when you came in?"

"Because I had to turn on the air conditioner and change and get ready for dinner. First things first."

She doesn't understand, and who can blame her. "What did shea say? When is shea cominga back?"

"I don't know."

"Why not?"

"Because she doesn't know."

"Did you aska her to comea back?"

"No. She'll come back when she's ready."

"I'll bet ifa you aska her, she'da come back."

Bill ignores this, instead saying "She's staying with a woman from work, someone named Jerry."

And his mother in law ignores this, of course, because she already knows where Helen is staying. "Did you aska her whatsa wrong."

"Yeah." He pauses for a moment. "She said she didn't know."

"Well, I already tolda you whatsa wrong, but you don'ta believea me."

"Yeah, yeah, yeah, I don't want to hear it."

"Of coursea you don't." He looks up at her and glares. The air conditioner has kicked in, and it feels like a vise is being twisted around Bill's chest. He wants to lash out at this person living in his home, this person who's making his life a living hell. But he doesn't have the breath, or suddenly the inclination, to do it. Somewhere, Bill can hear the laughter. It's faint, but he can definitely hear it.

-24-

"Ha, ha, ha, ha, that was him?!" Jerry asks through her hilarity.

"Yeah, that was him," Helen answers sullenly. She's surprised Jerry is not angry about going to lunch with Bill. She would be, probably, if she hadn't run into him in the hallway.

"He looks like such a skinny little shit. And that big nose. I hope for your sake his dick is as big as his nose." Helen wants to tell Jerry to shut up, to stop talking about her husband like that, but she doesn't dare. Then her mood changes. "Does he know about us?"

"He knows I'm staying with you."

"That's not what I asked you," an angry Jerry goes on.

"No."

"I want you to tell him."

"I'm not ready."

"When will you be ready?"

Never is the answer, but she just tells Jerry she doesn't know. She could never tell Bill about Helen. It would crush him that some lesbian woman could satisfy her, when Bill wouldn't. Helen's leaving him was a big enough blow to his ego, he doesn't need this.

And apparently, he doesn't need her. If he did, he would have asked her to come back. But he never did. If he asked, Helen may have come back. But maybe she wouldn't. All Helen wants is some sign Bill still loves her, needs her, wants her. But he can't do it.

Helen wonders if Bill ever did need her. Need and love are two very different things. Helen needs Jerry, but she doesn't love her. And without love, the need will eventually go away. Helen always needed and loved Bill. But she needed Bill to need her in return, but he never did. And just like the need will go away without the love, the love will go away without the need. Jerry slaps Helen in the face. "Stop thinking about him!" Helen just sits there, stone faced. Not one tear comes to her eyes. Jerry's really not that strong, anyway, so it doesn't hurt all that much when Jerry hits her. Besides, after what Helen's going through, it'll take more than a slap in the face to hurt her. Jerry only does it because she loves her. And the thought of Helen going back

to Bill drives Jerry crazy. Love is a funny thing. It drives you to all kinds of extremes. It drives Jerry to hit Helen. And it drove Helen away from Bill.

-25-

"Would you like to go to lunch?" Finally, after weeks of torturing him, Sarah has finally asked him to go to lunch. Finally, they will get to talk, and get the ball rolling on their inevitable affair. But when he looks up, it's not Sarah giving him that sexy, come hither look, but his boss Sally Clamp. A clearly disappointed Bill asks "Why?" And an even more disappointed Sally says there are things she would like to talk to him about. Sure, lunch is fine. What choice does he have?

What could she want to talk to Bill about? It's got to be about work. Maybe she heard the conversation Bill had on the phone last week, in that one instance he forgot the tapes were rolling. Bill, frustrated that he hadn't made a sale in the previous few days, bullied a teenager into changing her family's long distance service from Sprint to M.C.I. Maybe the mother called the phone company, who in turn called M.C.I., who in turn called Bill's company, who tracked it down to him, and they were listening and re-listening to the tapes even as we speak. Yeah, that must be it. Bill is probably getting fired at lunch.

Unless she wants to talk about Sarah. She and Sarah have been pretty chummy these days. They must talk about him when they are at lunch. And Sarah must have told him about Helen. And

Sarah must have professed her love for him, and maybe Sarah told Sally that she should tell Bill to ask Sarah out. And Sally is only helping out her new friend. Yeah, that must be it. This lunch will lead to Bill and Sarah finally taking the proverbial roll in the hay. Unless, of course, Sally fires him.

Sarah walks up to Bill, as he exchanges smiles and frowns on his face as he contemplates his lunch date with his boss. "So, you and Sally are going to lunch." Word travels fast.

A proud Bill answers "Yes. Yes I am."

"Do you know what she wants to talk to you about?"

"No." And then he adds "Why, do you?"

"How would I know?," she answers with a sly smile. Like hell she doesn't know. Bill watches as Sarah walks away, obviously displaying her pretty round ass for him. Bill smiles, as he's sure he'll soon be pounding away at that body, rather than just at the thought of it.

Bill and his boss Sally Clamp enter the Japanese restaurant with a flow of other lunchers. They are hustled to a small table in a corner. Bill waits for Sally to sit down, presumably in the seat with the wall behind it. But Sally takes the other chair, the chair where one can comfortably move his or her chair back. So Bill squeezes himself into the other chair, his stomach hitting the table, his back up against the wall. Just as they settle in, another waiter shoves menus in their hands. "The place is kind of hectic," Sally observes. You picked it, Bill thinks. Bill hates Japanese food. Either it's raw, maggot-infested fish, or it's horsemeat covered with salty gross teriyaki sauce. But Sally loves Japanese food, and you can't disobey the boss when she's about to place the girl of your dreams in your lap. "So I guess you're wondering what I want to talk to you about." Before Bill has a chance to answer, the waiter comes back. "Ready to order." It was a command, not a question. Before Bill has a chance to say he hasn't even looked at their bacteria-laden menu, Sally says "I'll order for us." And she proceeds to do just that, ordering lunch for Bill that he hopes doesn't taste as bad as it sounds. "And one more thing, can you turn the air conditioner up? It's kind of hot in here."

"So anyway, there's one bit of unpleasantness I'd like to get out of the way before lunch." Bill assumes she wants to change a tampon or something, but it's nothing of the kind. "I got a call yesterday from an angry M.C.I. representative." Uh oh. "She said an even angrier woman called her, saying her daughter decided to change the family's long distance service. To make a long story short, I pulled the tape." She takes an audio cassette out of her pocketbook.

Bill can only shake his head at his own stupidity. "I'll clean out my desk when I get back."

"There's no need to do that." And with that, she holds out the tape to Bill. "I took care of the whole thing. None of the other bosses know. Here, take it." Bill slowly reaches out to take it, just like Moses presumably slowly reached out to take the hot coal instead of the gold, and putting it in his mouth, forever impeding his ability to speak properly, so that his brother Aaron had to do all the talking for him, so "Let My People Go" wouldn't sound like "Le Mu Puhpe Gu," and the Pharoah would know what the hell they were talking about. "I don't have to tell you not to do something like this again, so I won't. End of subject." Bill looks down at the tape, a tape that could have ruined his life. And he looks up at the woman, a woman who is responsible for saving what's left of his stupid life.

"Thank you."

"I don't want to discuss it ever again." Bill slips the tape into the breast pocket of his shirt. After a short pause to compose herself, Sally says "So now that that's out of the way..." But before she can talk, the food comes. The dumpling appetizer comes at the same time as the main course. Two waiters jabbering in Japanese are rearranging the salt and pepper and the dreadful teriyaki sauce that's already on the table, so they can fit the rest of the plates on the miniscule table. Bill's cool Ray Bans, which up until now have been sitting comfortably in their case on the table have now been pushed against the wall by the Japanese man. Fearing they will be broken by further pressure, Bill takes them, and goes to place them in his breast pocket. But the tape is already there, so he simply places his sunglasses on his lap. In what seemed and probably was an instant, the table is filled with plates of all sorts of strange looking items. Bill wants to back away from the table just a bit, just in case any of these culinary delights decide to move, but of course, he's locked in between wall and table. Sally begins to talk, saying something about herself and relationships and the like, but Bill is busy arranging the napkin on his lap, trying to smooth it out as much as he can, considering his sunglasses are making an annoying lump. Bill recognizes a dumpling as one he has seen in Chinese restaurants, so he takes a fork and skewers it. But what's inside is completely foreign to Bill. What should be pork is some sort of green oozing slime. As Sally is talking about her first husband, she sees Bill is looking puzzled at the dumpling. "It's liquified squid." Great. Bill cleans out the dumpling, and eats the dough. Sally just watches and smiles. "You know, you're delightful." Sally finally says.

Bill looks up. "Me?"

"Yes, you. Don't act like you don't know it. It's just fun to watch you, watch you clean out a dumpling and eat just the dough. It's adorable. You're adorable. You're so unlike my ex-husband."

"You were married?"

"Yes. I was just telling you that."

"Oh. I guess I wasn't listening." Sally gently lifts up a dumpling with her chopsticks. Show off. Bill decides to cut to the chase. "So you and Sarah have been getting pretty friendly lately."

"Why bring her up?"

"No reason. I just noticed you guys have been going to lunch together every day for the past few weeks."

"Are you jealous that I'm taking your lunch partner away?"

"Jealous? Why would I be jealous?"

"Enough about her." Bill is suspiciously eyeing this tri-colored goo on one of the plates, and decided to take a shot at it. "It's-" Sally starts to say, but Bill cuts her off.

"Don't tell me, or I won't eat it." It eases down Bill's throat. Not too bad.

"Actually, Sally says, "Japanese food's quite healthy. Although it doesn't appear to be, it's really very good for you."

"A lot of things are like that."

"No kidding." They eat together in relative silence, except for Sally's laughter as Bill dissects his meal. The waiters keep looking over, hoping to clear the table for the next wave of lunchers. Bill sees this, and it makes him uneasy. His inability to move his chair also makes him uncomfortable, as does the increased cold air which Sally requested, binding his lungs.

"You know, I really don't know why you like her."

"Like who?" Bill is startled by the sudden break in the comforting silence.

"Sarah."

"Who says I like her?"

"It's obvious."

"I mean, of course I like her. We're friends. But that's it."

"Oh really?"

"Yes, oh really. Anyway, I'm not the one who's been prancing off to lunch with her every day for the past three and one half weeks."

"Have you been keeping track?"

"No." The answer is really yes. Sally is starting to annoy Bill.

"In any case," Sally says, "I'm really not all that fond of her. She really is quite selfish. And she doesn't open up and tell you anything about her, but yet when you open up to her, she really isn't listening. And if she is listening, it doesn't seem like she cares."

"Then why go to lunch with her every day?"

"I could ask you the same question."

"But you didn't. I asked you."

"Well..." Here it comes. Say it. Sarah is the one asking you to go to lunch, so you will tell me to ask her out. Say it. Say it. "I'm using her."

"YOU'RE using HER?"

"Yes, she's got something I want, and I want to learn from her how to get it."

"Oh yeah, what's that?," a suddenly bored and disinterested Bill asks.

"You."

"Heh?" Bill is suddenly interested again.

"Yes, you."

"Well," Bill stammers, "this is a surprise."

"It shouldn't be. I've been dropping hints for months."

"I'm bad with hints."

"Apparently."

"And I guess when Sarah told you my wife left me, you figured now was a good time to make your move?"

"Your wife left you?!"

"Yeah. You didn't know?"

"No."

"You mean, you spent all that time talking to Sarah about me, and she didn't tell you that?"

"No." Bitch, thinks Sally. Interesting, thinks Bill.

After a long time, with the table already cleared, with the check sitting there, and the waiters waiting, Sally Clamp asks, "Well, what do you think?"

"I don't know. This is so sudden."

"Well, think about it. And think about how much I've done for you." Bill thinks about what's in his breast pocket. He can only smile. Sally learned from the master.

-26-

Mr. Sally Clamp. It has a nice ring to it. He'd be well respected in the company, married to one of the up and coming executives. He'd never have to worry about his job. He can spend the rest off his life on the phone with idiots, trying to sell them crap. Yep, life never looked so good.

Sally is a handsome looking woman, Bill thinks as he looks over his shoulder to get onto the highway. Sure, she's a little chunky, and sure, she's got small breasts, and sure, she's got eyes that bug out and one of those pig noses, and sure, she's got fat ankles, but other than that, very very lovely.

What's Bill supposed to do now? When they left the restaurant, they didn't make any plans to date or anything. Is Bill supposed to ask her to dinner or the movies, or are they supposed to fly to Las Vegas, get Bill a quicky divorce, and then just get married?

And what about Sarah? How does she fit into all of this? Why would Sarah help Sally to get Bill, when Sarah is supposed to want Bill? And if Sarah was indeed trying to help Sally get Bill, why wouldn't Sarah tell Sally that Helen left Bill? All of this thinking, all of these names, is giving Bill a headache. Bill's been getting headaches every night now, but they usually start when he gets home, and sees his mother in law in the kitchen in her loose fitting garments, the sweat dripping down the back of her neck. Or sometimes she's in the living room, smoking a cigarette, the cigarette to her mouth, taking a deep breath, taking all of the smoke in, then slowly exhaling.

Or are Bill and Sally just supposed to just have sex? God, Bill hasn't had sex in months. He thought the next time would be with sexy skinny Sarah, but it looks like its going to be with saggy sucky Sally. Whatever. Bill hasn't had an orgasm for some time now, unless you count those dreams that Bill would not like to think about. His plumbing's all backed up. The next time he comes, he'll probably bust the condom, the force will be so large, as will the quantity. So Sally or Sarah, Sarah or Sally, it doesn't really matter anymore.

Bill wonders what Helen's doing for sex. Masterbating, probably, with that vibrator Bill found in Helen's drawer. Helen said the girls at the office bought it for her as a gag gift for her birthday, and that she never used it, but Bill didn't believe her. Because he smelled it, and he could smell her sweet juices. He even licked it, and could get a faint taste of it. But still, she denied it. He begged and pleaded with her to use it while they were having sex, but she refused, saying the thought of that thing inside her made her want to be sick. One time, though, in an effort to revive their dying sex life, Bill secretly took the thing out, and started putting it inside Helen while he was eating her. But the instant it touched her labia, she knew what it was. She went crazy. She jumped up and started screaming. It took an hour to calm her down. Bill never tried that again. In fact, that was the last time Bill tried anything with Helen.

Bill pulls up to his house. But he can't go in, he can't face the Disagreeable Widow, not this night. So he quickly backs out and takes off, before she can see him. But she's already standing at the door, watching him, smiling. Without the air conditioner on, she can hear everything.

Bill begins to drive, aimlessly at first, just weaving in an out of the residential blocks in his neighborhood, slowing down so as to avoid crushing the children playing stickball on the sweltering asphalt. There's nowhere for him to go, really, nowhere for him to go alone. So he drives, thinking about nothing in particular, just the car's annoying pulling to the right, and what turn to take next.

Suddenly though, Bill has a rare urge. He wants a beer. Bill was never a big drinker, and never liked beer, except for a brief time in college. But suddenly, a beer sounds pretty good. He knows about this local establishment where some people hang out. He and Helen never went there. They were not the types for bars.

But Bill often thought about this place. Thought about going there alone one night, and meeting a beautiful woman, whom he would take home, to whom he would make love all night long.

He walks into the place, sits down at the bar, and orders a beer. He looks around. Not many people in here. There are two guys playing pool at the bar's lone pool table. A couple sits in one of the booths, staring into each other's eyes, and taking shots of Absolute. Another guy sits alone at the other end of the bar. And there's a woman, also alone, a few barstools down.

These local pubs are quiet places early on a Tuesday night. Bill has driven by late on Fridays and Saturdays, and he can hear the place from the road, and see the overspilling crowd outside, drinking and carrying on. But tonight there are the diehards, those few who have to have a drink before going home, or who just need a place to go because they can't go home, or who have no one else but the bartender to talk to.

Bill sips his beer slowly. After all these years, it still tastes and smells like urine to him. Why he got the urge to drink a beer he'll never know. He looks at the woman at the bar. She looks 30ish, with long hair that may be a little too long for her age, jeans and a white t-shirt which she fills out quite well, and a sad look to her eyes. Bill stares, wondering why they are so sad.

"Whaddaya lookin at?" she asks when she just can't take the relentless staring anymore. Years ago, it never bothered her, it happened so often.

"Uh, nothing. You just look familiar is all."

"Well, you don't know me," she says as she throws her head back, and smooths out the back of her hair. Yes, he does know her. Those tell-tale motions tell Bill the woman he's looking at is none other than Stacy Wellman, the girl he and every other boy going through puberty in high school lusted after.

"Stacy Wellman."

She rolls her eyes. Great. She'll have to hear another guy tell her how he lusted after her in high school, and he was too shy to talk to her, but now, here they are, more than ten years later, so..."Yeah, you caught me. Which one were you?"

"Bill Press. Billy Press."

A genuine look of recognition comes over her face. "Yeah, I remember you. You used to stare at me in math class. You always seemed like a sweet kid." Bill smiles. "A little nerdy, but sweet." Bill frowns.

"Yeah, that was me, sweet but nerdy."

"And don't tell me. Now, you've changed."

Bill would love to think that's true, but it's not. "Not all that much, unfortunately." Stacy drains the rest of her drink, gets up and moves over to the stool next to Bill. The bartender quickly gives her a fresh new drink. For the first time in more than a decade, Bill is able to get a good look at the first girl who ever gave him an erection. My, how the years have changed her. If her face wasn't indelibly marked in his mind from those hours of staring, he never would have recognized her. It's still Stacy, but the face has lines, the hips are a little wider, and those eyes, oh those sad eyes.

"You're married I see." She looks at his wedding ring.

"Um, yeah, you?"

"No." The eyes grow sadder.

"I'm sorry" is all Bill can think of to say.

She downs another drink. "Don't pity me. I'm Stacy Wellman, the prettiest girl in school. It's your fault, you know. You and your little schoolbuddies. Staring at me all of the time, having to hear that this guy likes me and that

guy likes me. No one was good enough for me, Stacy Wellman." The bartender brings her another drink, which she quickly drains as well. "But as much as I blame you guys, I can't complain. Men have been so good to me, or at least they used to be, when I still had my girlish looks. But women, oh women do indeed suck. They're never happy. And if they are happy, don't worry, they'll find a reason to be unhappy, you bet you me. I passed up so many men, because I was Stacy Wellman, the prettiest girl in school, and they just were not good enough for me. I played games with them. They thought I loved them, then I just dumped them, because something better came along." She pauses to take a swig of her latest drink. "Billy Press. Sweet but nerdy, but lucky. He loves his wife, his wife loves him, and they live happily ever after. You can't live in the past, no matter how good it was. Billy Press. First term trigonometry. I remember him. Nice boy." Bill waves off what would have been Stacy's next drink. He pays for his beer (it appears Stacy has a tab at this place), and props Stacy on her feet. He begins to lead her out, but first he takes off his wedding ring, and puts it in the ashtray, joining a bunch of used cigarette butts and old gum. He hears the sound of laughter. He turns around, but everyone in the bar is stonefaced.

-27-

Unfortunately for Bill, the first office he has to walk by in order to get to his work station belongs to his boss Sally Clamp. Or should he say, his girlfriend Sally Clamp. Bill stops before he is in view of her open door. If he walks by really fast, maybe she won't see him. So he backs up a few steps, to get a running start. It only takes two strides before he gets to her door, and just like you have to smell the milk even though you know it's sour, he has to slow down, to see if she's in there. Of course she is, where else would she be? She sees him. He begins to speed up again, but it's no use. "Hey Bill, where are you running?"

Without entering the office, he says, "Oh, I thought I heard my phone ringing."

"Don't worry. Someone else will get it. Come in." So he goes in. "So, have you given any thought to what we discussed yesterday?"

"Uh, yeah."

"And?"

"And what?"

"What are we going to do?"

"I dunno."

"Well, the ball is in your court. It's entirely up to you. If you don't want to, well, I'd understand. But, you know, I've done so much for you…" Bill looks around the office. There has got to be a copy of that tape around here somewhere. She wouldn't give him the only one. She's not that dumb. Remember from whom she learned. "So, what do you think?" The sweat begins to drip off Bill's forehead. "You're sweating. I'll tell them to turn the air conditioner up."

She reaches for the phone, but Bill stops her. "No, that's all right." She puts the phone down, and saunters over to Bill. "Then let me take care of it for you." Sally then stands on her tip-toes, and licks the sweat off Bill's forehead. "There, now isn't that better?" Bill runs out of the office, and makes it to the bathroom in time to wretch last night's beer and little else into the toilet. He gets up and washes his face with cold water, then pumps the soap dispenser several times, and scrubs his forehead. He washes it off and dries it, but still he can smell Sally's sour saliva. He scrubs again and again, until his forehead is beet-red, and free of Sally. He again attempts to walk past her office, but there she is, standing at the door. "Are you all right?"

But Bill just looks at her, and walks away. Sally smiles. She loves him so.

Bill gets to his desk, and puts on his headset. Sarah walks by. "Hey Sarah." She looks at his red forehead, gives him a sly smile, and walks away. Bill throws off his headset, and follows her. "Sarah, Sarah," but she doesn't turn around. She gets to her desk, and sits down. "What's up?" She shrugs. "Listen, we haven't gone to lunch together in weeks. Do you want to go today?"

"Aren't you going with Sally."

"No."

"Don't you think you should?"

"Fuck Sally Clamp."

Sarah smiles. "Sure, I'd love to go to lunch with you."

Virtually every day, the thermometer has been above 90. You can see the heat rising off the street. You can see it in the faces of people as they trudge along, you can see how hot and tired everyone is, how they just wish it would all go away. They pray for winter, with its snow and sub-freezing temperatures. And when that comes, they pray for summer, to melt it all away. But the summer comes, and its no relief. It never ends, this misery.

Needless to say, Bill shares in this misery. He sweats when he's outside, he can't breathe when he's inside. Bill prays for autumn, then spring. He doesn't like the extremes. Fall and spring are just fine with him. Spring, when the leaves come to life, for a short, brief shining moment, to shelter us during the harsh summer, but go away gracefully in autumn, before the terrible winter deals them a painful death.

Sarah decides she wants to eat outside in this horrible weather, so they grab a couple of sandwiches, and head to a park bench. While Sarah just plops right down, Bill wipes the presumably filthy bench off before sitting. Homeless people probably drooled there overnight. They unwrap their sandwiches. Sarah opted for the Italian hero of salami, baloney, and pepperoni with lettuce, tomato, and Italian dressing, while Bill went for the roast beef and ham, with lettuce, tomato, and mayonnaise. Sarah dives right in, the dressing leaking out onto the wax paper spread out on the bench. Bill's wax paper is on his lap, not wanting his sandwich in any close proximity to the bench. He takes a bite, puts down his sandwich, and reaches for his napkin to wipe his mouth and hands. But there's no napkin for which to reach. "Can I have a napkin?"

"I gave you one," Sarah answers with food in her mouth. Bill remembers. He used it to wipe the bench.

"Are there any more?" Sarah nods her head no. There is one, though, and it's draped across Sarah's leg. She's not using it. She never uses her napkin. "What about that one?" He points to Sarah's napkin.

"That's mine." So, Bill thinks, you're a slob. I'm the neat guy. But Sarah has no intention of parting with the napkin. So Bill, with a spot of mayonnaise on his hand, has to suck it off rather than wipe. Sarah also has no intention of starting a conversation. So Bill has to. "So, what's new?"

"Nothing." Of course.

Bill sits for a while, trying to think of something to say. "So, how are The Hamptons?"

"Great." She looks up and smiles. A piece of salami is stuck to her lip. She licks it off with her tongue, rather than using the virgin napkin. Bill would have wiped.

"Go there often?"

"Every weekend."

"So, you and Sally have been getting pretty chummy lately."

"You and her, too, from what I hear."

"What is it you hear?" Bill asks defensively.

"Oh, I just hear she's got her eye on you." Not just her eye, as Bill's still throbbing forehead indicates.

"I'm sure you heard it directly from her." He wants to strangle Sarah for playing these games. He has the urge to kiss her, too.

"Well, girls do talk, you know." Bill takes another bite of his sandwich. He wants to wipe, but there's nothing to wipe on. His hands are getting all greasy from residual cold cut oils that are on the bread. He's even transferring the invisible oils to his soda can.

"Well, when you girls talk, what do you talk about?"

"Oh you know, girl stuff."

"Guys?"

"Sure."

"Me?"

"Um, no, I can't recall your name ever coming up." Liar, who else would they talk about? He's Bill Press, the best seller at Prevail Marketing. He's the only thing these two women have in common. Except, that is, they have their female parts in common. They have that glue that binds them forever. However different Sarah and Sally are, and any woman for that matter, they are women, and they have that bond. Women look at each other as they walk down the street.

They pretend to look at their clothing, but Bill knows they are giving each other the secret look, that look that says "I acknowledge the fact that you are in the sorority of women, that if need be, I can call upon you at any time, as we continue to take the world away from the men." Men can't do that. Give a man some kind of look, and he'll think you're a homo or weird or something. Bill is angry Sarah is not telling him the truth. He wants to know why she didn't tell Sally that Helen left Bill. And the frustration is growing inside him that he can't wipe his hands. He's choking his sandwich down, just so he can be done with it, so he can go to a water fountain and wash his hands. He continues to eye the unused napkin on Sarah's lap. Why won't she give it to him if she's not going to use it?

"What do you think of Sally?" Bill asks.

"She's all right. Why, thinking of dating her?"

"No."

"Yeah, sure," she says sarcastically.

"I'm not." Bill is angry.

Sarah remains composed. "All right. Don't get mad at me. You say you don't want to date her, fine, you don't. I couldn't care less." With that, she takes the last bite of her sandwich, picks up the unused napkin, and simply tosses it into the waxpaper, crumples it up, and throws it into the nearby trash can. Now Bill's blood is really beginning to boil. His hands are filled with roast beef and ham with lettuce, tomato and mayonnaise, and Sarah won't tell him the truth. God, how he hates her. "So, when are you coming out to The Hamptons?"

"Huh."

"Remember, I invited you? You're welcome anytime. Just give me a few days notice." So she won't have to buy a train ticket in advance. Since Bill has a car, for one weekend anyway, she doesn't have to put up with that dreadful train station.

"Uh, yeah, I'll let you know."

"Great. Let's go." She gets up, and starts walking away while Bill crumples up his waxpaper and cleans his area. He can still catch a glimpse of her as he waits on line at the water fountain to wash his hands.

-28-

Helen just throws her clothes into her suitcase. She's got to get out of here, before she's caught. What is she doing here? She can't believe she ever lived here. What kind of life was this? Being miserable every day, wishing she was somewhere else, somewhere she belonged. Fortunately, Helen knows where she belongs. She knew it all along. And that's where she's going after she gets all of her stuff out of this place.

What was she doing here all this time? Living with a person who doesn't treat her with respect, who doesn't listen to what she says, to whom she must be subservient. Looking back on her time here, it's as though she lived through a nightmare.

She hears a noise. Is work over already? She can't be caught here doing this, because all hell will break loose. But it was just the neighbor coming home. She looks around at this room, at the room they used to make love in so much. She can't remember any of it, except the last time, because she knew it would be the last time. It wouldn't have been so bad if she didn't know that. Just like Dostoevsky said in "Crime and Punishment," the death penalty is indeed the worst way to die. Because as you're being walked to the electric chair, you know with absolute certainty you are going to die. You know the governor's not going to call. At least people facing a lethal situation, like a drowning or a mugging at gunpoint, can keep in the back of their mind that maybe they'll get out of this alive. There is still that ray of hope, however dim in might be. For Helen, that last time was the darkest time of her life.

But she can rest assured that such a grim sexual encounter will never happen again. She's sure now. She's going back where she belongs. She'll never enter this place again. Helen leaves a note on the dresser, picks up the heavy bag, and proceeds to the front door. She looks back, fondly at first, then in anger, then fondly again. There were some good times in this place, some horrible times, too. But there's no time to be sentimental. She's got to get out of here, before Bill comes home.

Bill looks at his left hand on the steering wheel. For the first time in 6 years, there is no ring on his finger. There is a white line going around the bottom of his ring finger, a remnant of the 6 years the ring protected his finger from the elements. Bill wonders if it will ever go away, wonders if it will remain with him forever, a constant reminder of his failure.

He also wonders why he did it. He wasn't drunk. He hardly touched his beer, listening to Stacy Wellman tell her sad story with those eyes of hers. She wanted him to stay last night. She promised to make all of his teenaged fantasies come true. She begged him not to leave her alone. God, how tired she is of being alone. But Bill just couldn't. He kept looking down at his ring finger, but the ring was gone, it could offer no excuse. But looking at the beautiful Stacy Wellman in her current state, he just couldn't conjure up those old feelings about her. That was in the past, so many years ago. So he left, left her sobbing in her bed. So sad.

Bill is thinking about the ring, thinking about wanting to get it back. He always wondered what he would do with it if Helen died. Eventually, he'd have to get on with his life, and that would mean taking the ring off. In Bill's mind, that would have been the hardest thing to do. The ring meant so much. He speculated he'd put it on his key ring, so it would always be with him. So that he could look at it any time he wanted, and read the inscription "With this ring I thee wed." And now it's in the landfill, or maybe the bartender fished it out of the dirty ashtray, and is holding it just in case someone accidentally dropped it in there. He'll hold it for 30 days, then he'll probably sell it to some cheap place, where it will inevitably wind up on the finger of some poor person, who manages to scrape up enough money to buy a used ring for himself and his bride. They won't be matching, though, unless Helen ditches her ring, and they somehow end up together.

What if Helen does come back, and they remain married for all of eternity? What does he do then about his ring? He can always say he lost it, and go out and get another one made. He hopes that is what will happen. He hopes he stays married to Helen. That is what he wants. He knows for sure. He wants to have to go out, and inscribe a ring "With this ring I thee wed." And then the date of their marriage: August 3. It doesn't even occur to Bill that yesterday was his sixth wedding anniversary.

"You didn'ta coma homa until late lasta night," his mother in law said as he walks through the door.

"No, I didn't."

"I wasa expecting that. But I wasa also expecting Helen to bea homa today."

"Why?" Bill asks as he closes all of the windows and flicks on the air conditioner.

"You have to aska why?"

"Apparently, yes," an exasperated Bill answers.

"It wasa youra anniversary yesterday."

Bill pauses. "I know."

"Then why didn't youa call her?"

"I did."

"She saysa you didn't."

"Well, I called and she was away from her desk. And I don't have her number where she's staying. Do you?"

"No." His mother in law figures if Bill can lie, then so can she. "I thoughta you anda she would spend a romantic anniversary together, and you'da get back together."

"Well, it didn't happen. But don't worry. Helen will be coming back soon."

"I don'ta thinka so."

Bill explodes. "Of course you don't think so! You think you know fucking everything. Well, you don't." Having effectively put his mother in law in her place, Bill goes upstairs to his bedroom. Something looks different. It

suddenly looks empty, even though all of his stuff is still crammed onto Helen's side of the bed. He sees the note. "I took the rest of my things. I think it's best that way. Helen." Maybe his mother in law is right. Maybe Helen is not coming back any time soon. Maybe he should go downstairs and apologize to her. Instead, he takes off his clothes and goes to bed. He falls asleep quickly. He sleeps soundly.

"Hey Bill, come on down for dinner." The bellowing of his mother in law wakes him up. Was he sleeping? How did that happen? Yeah, yeah, he yells down. It's awfully cold in the house. The air conditioner has never worked that well.

He puts on a pair of pants and a shirt, and heads downstairs. As he hits the middle of the stairway, though, it suddenly turns hot. It's so hot, steam seems to be rising from the carpeting. Or are his eyes still cloudy from sleep? Either way, he has trouble seeing through it. "Bill, come on down," he hears her saying. Bill gets to the bottom of the stairs. Still, he can't see anything through the haze. He walks to the middle of the living room, and it all clears up. And there is his mother in law, lying naked on the couch, sweat pouring off of her brow, beads of perspiration forming on her large breasts, and dripping down into her armpit. She has an ice cube in her hand, running it up and down her body. It starts at her mouth, where she licks it, and then proceeds through her cleavage, and down her torso, where it stops just above her clitoris. She arches her back in pleasure when it gets there. "Come to me." He doesn't want to, but a naked Bill does what he's told. He is fully erect. "Come and fuck me." Bill starts to breathe heavily. He is both excited and repelled at the same time. His penis starts to ache. "Come and fuck me." She spreads her legs wide open, and Bill enters. It feels so hot, it feels so good. But then Helen screams "Get that out of me!" Bill wakes up, shaking. It was just one of those dreams again.

-29-

Getting clean these days is becoming increasingly harder for Bill. The heat, and those frightful dreams which cause him to wake up in a sweat, are making his secret bar of soap work overtime in the shower each morning. The bar is still about half its original size. It's amazing how long soap lasts when only one person uses it. The paper in which it is wrapped is getting quite soggy and disgusting. But who is Bill to take the soap away from its original wrapper?

However miserable his life is, however lousy Sarah treats him, however much Sally Clamp wants him to be her boyfriend, however much his mother in law aggravates him, however much Helen won't tell him what's wrong, there's always his soap. It is his, and his alone. No one can take it away from him. Sarah can't make his soap treat him poorly, Sally Clamp can't use it to blackmail him, his mother in law can't make it hard and short like her stupid pasta, and Helen can't even begin to assume something is wrong with it. It's clean and pure, 99 1/4 percent anyway. It's his salvation, really. It's what keeps him going. All this, from a little white bar of soap, that somehow manages to clean away what's wrong in Bill's world.

"Bill, we need to talk," says the thing that's REALLY wrong in his world.

"Yes, Sally."

"Well, it's been two weeks."

"Two weeks since what?"

"I have to tell you?"

"No, you don't."

"So, have you filed for divorce yet?"

"No."

"What are you waiting for?"

"I never said we're getting a divorce. We're just separated."

"Hmm. Well, what about me?"

"What about you?"

"What becomes of me if you don't get divorced?"

"I don't know."

"Here's another question. What becomes of me if you DO get divorced?"

"I don't know."

"Well, you should."

"What do you mean 'I should'?"

"Just that you should."

"Are you going to tell me?"

"No." Another one, Bill thinks. He turns to leave, but Sally says, "Oh, Bill. congratulations on those sales numbers last week."

"What do you mean? I had a lousy week last week."

"No you didn't." She gives him a sly smile, one of those Sarah smiles. "You were the top seller once again at Prevail Marketing. The big-wigs were very pleased. They said they're happy to have the old Bill Press back. And they congratulated me, figuring I did a lot to motivate you. Remember that. You'll always do well here, as long as I'm around."

"That wasn't necessary," Bill finally says.

"Oh, yes it was." Indeed, it was.

Bill walks out, and waiting at his desk is Sarah. "So, it looks like Labor Day weekend," she says.

"Excuse me?"

"It looks like that weekend is when you'll be coming out to The Hamptons with me."

"Why so late?" Bill hadn't given it much thought. Although it's been the only thing on his mind, going out to The Hamptons, seeing Sarah in her bikini, making love to her all night long. But actually when this would happen, actually making the plan, was not on Bill's agenda.

"Because, that's the next time I'm going out. I have things to do here in town for the next few weekends. So, you're coming Labor Day."

"Yeah, sure." That means canceling his annual Labor Day barbecue, which Bill guesses was cancelled anyway, what with his separation from Helen, and considering everyone who was invited were friends of Helen's from work or old friends from high school. Those Labor Day barbecues were always fun times for Bill. Joking and flirting with Helen's girlfriends, but more important, he could celebrate the survival of another treacherous summer, when the heat threatened to melt away the very existence of Bill's life. But always he defeated it. Until this year, that is. "No problem," he tells Sarah.

"Good. You'll drive."

"Yeah."

Good, thinks Sarah.

Just as Sarah walks away, Bill's phone rings. "Hello, Prevail Marketing."

"Bill?"

"Yes."

"It's Helen."

It's been so long since he's talked to her on the phone, he didn't even recognize her voice. "Hi."

"What's the matter, you don't even know your own wife's voice?"

"Sure I do."

"Whatever. Listen, how are you."

"Fine."

"It's been a while since we've talked. You know our anniversary came and went and you didn't even call me."

"I know. I was going to call you, but I don't have your number wherever it is you're staying, and I was too busy to call you at work from my work."

"Well, you could have called the next day."

"Hey, you could have called me too you know. You have my home number."

"I was waiting for you to call me. I was hoping you wouldn't confirm what I already know."

"And what's that?"

"You still don't know, do you?"

"Know what?"

"What our problem is."

"I guess not. Are you going to tell me?"

"No."

"Well then, I guess this conversation is over."

"What's the matter? Afraid to talk to me? Afraid you might figure it out?"

"I'm not afraid of anything."

Helen manages a chuckle amidst the tears. "You're deathly afraid. It's a scary thing."

"I don't know what you're talking about."

"And that's scary too." Helen hangs up. Bill listens to the dial tone in his headset for a while. He wanted to keep talking to Helen. He really did. But quite frankly, he had nothing really to say.

What a morning, and he's only been in work ten minutes. The air conditioner starts to kick in now, and Bill's chest tightens. They must have turned the thermostat up, because the pressure on Bill's chest is nothing like he's ever felt before. He can close his eyes, and visualize the air trying to get to his lungs, but the passageway is closing, allowing only a bit of air in at a time. At times like these, Bill is actually thankful his mother in law is living with him, turning off the air conditioner, steaming up the place, and allowing him to breathe freely again.

-30-

Helen reaches in the back of her drawer. Deep in the back, underneath her winter sweaters. That's where she keeps it, still in it's original box. The girls at work did give it to her as a gag gift, after they found out at a drunken office party that she had never masterbated. Helen howled when they gave it to her, and she threw it into a drawer at home, and never told Bill about it. He'd probably want to use it on her. And that would be too sick. That's why she hides it from Jerry, too.

It sat in that drawer for a couple of years. She had completely forgotten about it. But a few months ago, she was clearing out some old clothes when she stumbled upon it. Helen smiled as she took it out of the box. She looked at it. The fake gold still shining brightly on the outside. It was slippery. She knew it would go right in after she lubricated herself with some K-Y Jelly. She and Bill had used so much of that stuff during their marriage, they should have bought stock in the company.

By that point, it had been months since Bill touched her, so that gold vibrator in her hand was looking more and more desirable. No chance that it would go limp in the middle. No chance it would come after 20 seconds and not even care if she came. She sat there on the floor staring at it for what seemed like an eternity. She ran her hand up and down it. It was so smooth, not all veiny like a real one. It had a rounded end, like a bullet, which gradually got larger. It would fit so well. It was obviously designed by a woman. Helen could feel the tingling, could feel herself getting wet. For the first time ever, she put her hand down there. Bill was always trying to get her to touch herself during sex, but she never would. It would be disgusting. He also wanted to watch her masterbate, but that would be too sick. Her hand was wet now. It was almost slimy. Helen ran to the bathroom to wash. She put the vibrator away. She could never do anything like that.

That day seems like such a long time ago to Helen. She was such a different person. Now, it's nothing for her to masterbate. It's harder here at Jerry's because her schedule is so erratic. Bill was always home at the exact same time every single day, so Helen was able to pleasure herself and cook dinner before Bill was even close to being home.

Helen lies down on her back, naked, her trusty vibrator next to her on the bed. She rubs her breasts, and she smiles. Her hand slowly goes to her torso, to her already moist vagina. She puts her finger inside, arching her back. She takes her wet finger, and rubs just above her clitoris. She lets out a sigh. With her other hand, she reaches for the vibrator. She puts it in her mouth. She can still taste herself from yesterday. Or was it the day before? She sucks on it until it's drenched with her saliva. She lowers it now, rubbing it between her breasts, as she continues to work her clitoris. The vibrator goes lower, and without missing a beat, it takes the place of her hand. Helen brings her other hand up to her mouth, and licks her fingers. She loves the taste of herself. Sometimes at work, she'll go to the bathroom and get herself wet, just so she can taste her juices. She hates Jerry's taste. It's only her's she loves. With the vibrator wet and slippery, Helen lowers it a couple of inches, and slips it in her vagina. It goes all the way in. The fingers in Helen's mouth muffles a yell. It feels so good when it first goes in. She pushes it in and out, in and out. Then, Helen rolls over onto her stomach, and it goes in even deeper. With a flip of a switch at the base of it, Helen turns on the vibrator. The tingling sensation heightens. Helen's clitoris rubs on the bed. She's pushing it in harder and harder, deeper and deeper. She's rubbing on the bed faster and faster. She tries to hold back, to make it feel better, but she can't. The pressure is just took great, and Helen comes. She slows down now, her clitoris aching. She rolls over onto her back, and slowly removes the vibrator and turns it off. She brings it up to her mouth, and licks it off. After winding down, she puts it back in the box and puts it back in its drawer. She gets dressed. She thinks of Bill putting it inside her. She thinks of Jerry wanting to do God knows what with it if she found it. Maybe she'd even want to put it inside her own vagina. No. Never. This is for Helen's enjoyment, and her's alone. Not Bill's. Not Jerry's. Only her's.

"Bill. He'sa strangea guy."

"What do you mean?" Helen asks her mother. She invited her over tonight, because Jerry is supposed to be working late, then going out to some biker bar.

"I heara him screaming ata night somatimes."

"Screaming?"

"Yeah, suddenly he'lla wakea up, and scream, then go backa to sleep."

"He never used to do that."

"Maybe it'sa me," she says kiddingly, and they both laugh. "And also, he looksa ata me funny."

"Funny? You mean with hate in his eyes?"

"No. I can'ta explain it. It'sa not hate, it'sa certainly nota love. I don'ta know what it is. But he scares me sometimes."

"Oh, Bill would never do anything to hurt you."

"I know that. But somatimes...ah, forget it."

"What?"

"Nothing."

"Tell me." Helen is starting to get angry. How else is Bill abusing her mother?

"Well, somatimes he looksa ata me likea the boys back ina Sicily looked at me whena I was working on my daddy's farm."

"I don't follow."

"Alla thosea boys wanted was to pick upa by dress, and, well, youa know."

"Why would Bill look at you that way? You must be imagining things." God, Helen thinks, what depths did I drive this man to by leaving him?

"I don'ta know."

"Oh mom, don't worry about it."

"O.K., I won't." But she will, and so will Helen.

After a long pause, Helen asks, "Does Bill ever talk about me?"

"Nota really. He justa goes upastairs and watchesa baseball, and complains abouta the air condition. Whenever I talka about you anda him getting back together, he yells and goesa upastairs."

"Do you think he still loves me?"

She thinks for a moment. How can she break her daughter's heart. "Yes," she answers.

Helen now begins to cry. "Do you think he still wants me to move back?"

"Yes." Now her mother begins to cry. Helen looks at her wedding ring, the one she's still wearing, the identical one Bill left in an ashtray. "Do you wanta to comea back?" Helen breaks out in tears. So does her mother. They both know the answer.

Bill gets home, and much to his surprise, finds it cool, and empty. The note from his mother in law reads "Went to go out with my friends. Supper is in the refrigrater. I turn on the air condishun for you." Not bad for a third grade education. But how did she ever pass the citizenship test? Anyway, Bill unwraps the pasta and roast beef and mashed potatoes, and puts them in the microwave. He flips on the television, only to find nothing interesting on, so he turns it off. He also turns off the air conditioning. He hasn't been able to breathe all day, and he wants to be comfortable in his own home. The microwave is done, letting out a high pitched tone. With the house devoid of television or air conditioning noises, the tone is loud and clear, louder and clearer than Bill has ever heard. It almost pierces his entire being, it is so sharp. Fortunately, it stops, and he walks over to the table to eat, all the while listening to his feet first on the tile floor, then on the carpeting. He picks up his fork, and he can almost hear it leaving the paper napkin. He twirls his pasta on his fork, listening to the noodles splash with the sauce, as they form a perfect swirl on the utensil. He brings it to his mouth, and he can hear the sauce melting into the starchy pasta. The house is as quiet as it's ever been. It's both soothing and frightening. Is this what loneliness is? This solitary silence, where everything suddenly becomes clear to you? But at the same time, nothing is clear, because these noises distract you from everything else. These sounds are always there, but Bill could never hear them, because there was always someone there. Now Bill can hear the laughter. It's not coming from the microwave or the floorboards or his plate. But he can hear it. Bill starts to shake. He quickly turns on the television. "Wheel of Fortune" is on. It'll do, to drown out that horrible noise.

Helen and her mother are laughing, laughing for the first time since she arrived. For Helen, it's the first time she's laughed in months. Her mother is telling her impressions of Bill the first time she ever met him. They dated for months before Helen brought

Bill home to meet her mother and her now dead father. Helen
dreaded this, because she knew how disapproving they were of
any boy she dated. She preferred to go on as they were, with
Helen's parents not knowing they were dating, and Helen meeting
Bill at the movies or the mall or at miniature golf. But Bill insisted, he didn't want to live like this anymore. So she brought him
home. Bill rang the bell, Helen answered. They entered the living
room together, where Helen's mother and father were sitting,
waiting. To Bill, it seemed as though they had been sitting there
their whole life, waiting for the boy who would take their daughter away from them. Her mother tells Helen she remembers that
moment so clearly, it was as if it was yesterday, instead of a decade
ago. She says she took one look at Bill, standing next to her
daughter, and said to herself "She will never marry him." And the
ensuing conversation only confirmed that. Her mother says Bill
seemed cold to her, uncaring, unfeeling. Helen only musters a
smirk at this observation. Her mother says Bill didn't seem right
for her. Helen was so pretty, and Bill was skinny with glasses. And
then, the final blow to Bill: Her mother says she looked at Bill's
crotch, and you couldn't see anything. No outline, no nothing.
And she remembers thinking, Hey, it musta be true about Jewish
guys. And that's when they both break out in laughter. And they
are still laughing when Jerry walks in. They stop when Jerry slams
the door.

"Jerry. What are you doing here?" Helen is nervous when she
asks this.

"I came home early." Jerry is staring straight at Helen's mother
when she says this. "Who's this?"

"That's my mother. Mom, this is Jerry."

"Hello," her ever-so-polite mother says.

"Hi," is the response.

"So, won't you join us for some tea?"

"No, I'm just going to go to our room. Come with me. I'd like to talk to you," Jerry says to Helen.

"Okay. Mom, I'll just be a second." Her mother watches as Jerry leads Helen into the bedroom, and blinks when she slams the door behind them.

"What the hell is she doing here?"

"She's my mother. I'm allowed to have my mother over, aren't I?"

"Not without telling me. Who knows what you and your guests will do here."

"This is my mother. What am I going to do with her other than talk. Jerry, you're acting crazy."

Jerry walks right up to Helen, and points a finger in her face. "Never tell me I'm crazy. Understand. Never." Helen is frightened. She doesn't want Jerry to hit her while her mother is there. Helen easily covers up the marks with makeup for the next day at work. But she won't be able to work that magic right now. But Jerry doesn't hit her. Instead, she sits down on the bed, and dramatically changes her mood. "Talk. That's what I'm afraid of. She'll convince you to go back to that husband of yours. And that will leave me all alone."

Helen rushes over to her, and gets down on her knees at the foot of the bed. "Jerry, that will never happen. I'm never going back there."

"Yes you will. You'll leave me, just like you left him. You'll stop loving me, the way you stopped loving him.

Helen doesn't bother correcting her, and says "I'll never stop loving you."

"Prove it," Jerry says as she spreads her legs.

"Now? My mother's outside."

"If you really loved me, you would."

"I can't."

"Then get rid of her, and come back in here." So Helen gets up, and goes outside. She tells her mother Jerry's not feeling well, that she needs Helen to take care of her. Does Helen need any help? No thanks, Helen can do it on her own. Her mother leaves. When Helen gets back to the bedroom, Jerry is lying there naked, her legs spread wide open. Helen closes her eyes, puts her head between Jerry's legs. She begins to lick, her right eye wincing with each contact.

His mother in law walks into the house, to find Bill fully clothed on the couch, sleeping, with all the lights on, with one of those home shopping networks on the television. She runs to Bill. "Wakea up. Helen needsa you."

The sight of his mother in law standing over him as he is lying down frightens him, so he quickly sits up. "What?" He's still groggy.

"Helen needsa you."

"Why?"

"Listen, I'ma nota supposed to tella you, but I was witha Helen tonight."

Bill is indifferent to this bit of news. "So?"

"So, I talked to her. And she will comea back, if you aska her."

"She said that?"

"Not exactly."

"Then what exactly did she say?"

"I can'ta remember the exacta words, but that'sa what she meant."

Bill shakes his head. "I'm not going to ask her to come back. She'll come back when she's ready."

"No. She wantsa to know that you wanta her back."

"She knows I want her back."

"Do you tella her that?"

Bill hesitates. "Yeah, sure."

"Do you mean it when you tella her that?"

Bill begins to get angry. "Listen," he shouts. But then he stops. "I don't want to yell at you. I just want to go upstairs, and go to sleep." He starts to get up, but his mother in law stops him.

"There'sa somethinga else I want to tella you. And this isa why I say Helen needsa you." Bill had forgotten all about that opening comment.

"What."

"It'sa this person she'sa livinga with. Thisa Jerry."

"What about her?"

"Well, she'sa strange."

"Strange? In what way?"

"Well, she'sa like a man."

"You mean she looks and dresses like a guy."

"Yeah, and she acts likea one, too."

"What do you mean, 'she acts like one.'"

"I mean, I think she'sa gay."

Bill laughs. Anyone who looks a little different, his mother in law thinks is gay. "I'm sure she's not gay. But even if she is, big deal."

"It is a biga deal. You wanta Helen living with a gay?"

"Who cares? Helen's not gay, so what difference does it make? Now if you'll excuse me, I'm going upstairs."

"Listena Bill. I would never tella you whata to do. But I'ma tellinga you now. You got to geta her outta there, before it'sa too late."

"Too late?"

"Before she doesn'ta want to comea back. Before she findsa somaone else she wants."

Bill makes a disbelieving face. "Like who? Like this Jerry?"

"Maybe." Bill stands there for a moment. His chest begins to tighten up. Funny, the air conditioning is not even on. It's all so ridiculous. So he just goes up to his room, and goes to sleep. His mother in law, meanwhile, is also standing there. She doesn't understand. She doesn't understand how Bill can be so uncaring. She doesn't understand how one woman can have sex with another woman. But most of all, she doesn't understand why Helen and Jerry said those things in their bedroom, a conversation which could be partly heard by his mother in law through those thin apartment walls. But despite everything she doesn't understand, she can rest on the knowledge that she understands a lot more than Bill does.

-31-

Lesbian. Helen can't be lesbian, Bill thinks as he gets into his car to drive to work. If she was, though, it would explain a lot of things. Like why she didn't want to have sex with him. And why she went crazy when he put that vibrator inside her. Maybe it's all things hard that disgust her. Maybe she likes the soft touch of a labia on her tongue. Maybe she enjoys licking a wet vagina, sucking on a clitoris until it is hard, until it is almost bursting out of its protective hood. The thought of Helen being with another woman turns Bill on. Driving on the highway, he has his first non-Sarah erection in months.

Bill always wanted to bring another woman into bed with them. Helen always said no. She never even considered the idea. Now she may be doing it without him. This angers Bill. Hell, if she was going to do it, why not do it with him there? But as angry as he is, he's even more excited.

Unless she's doing it with some butch woman, like the woman he saw near the elevator that day at Helen's office. But Bill knows Helen, knows that if she's going to do something like that, she'd do it with a beautiful young woman, a tall blonde with huge breasts and a flat stomach. Bill can almost picture Helen nestled between the woman's luscious breasts.

But what is Bill thinking about? Helen is not gay. You just don't turn gay overnight. So maybe she is living with some dyke, but big deal. No way Helen is doing anything.

And what if she was? Would Bill instantly ask for a divorce? It's not like she's fucking some guy, another penis filling her hole, another guy's dick in her mouth, another guy's come she's swallowing. Bill suddenly gets another hard-on, his second on the trip to work, his second non-Sarah erection in months.

And how dare his mother in law tell him what to do, to get her out of there before it's too late. No one tells Bill Press what to do. Not his mother in law, not Helen, not Sarah, not Sally Clamp. Bill Press is a man. He does what he wants. The pressure on his chest has not stopped since last night. It's as if his lungs want to burst, yet he's having trouble forcing air into them.

Bill's car is his oasis. No one can reach him there. It's his time to be alone, but a good kind of alone, because it's only temporary, as temporary as Bill wants it to be. He can control everything in his car—the temperature, the radio, everything. And if Bill reaches his destination, and he's not ready to see anyone, he can just take a trip around the block, or even two. No one can reach him here, none of those women who are trying to wreck his life.

His life used to be so stable, so secure. Everything was the same, every day. There were no surprises. That's the way he liked it. In the past couple of months, everything has changed. Every day when he wakes up, he doesn't know what to expect. The only thing he can count on is that his bar of soap will be there for him. Funny, how one day you have a happy life and a happy marriage and a happy wife and a happy job, then the next day, all you have is soap. A bar of soap, that is shrinking and shrinking every day, until one day, it will be gone. It'll get so small, it'll slip out of your hands one day in the shower, and run down the drain, and be lost forever. That will be a sad day indeed. That day is coming soon for Bill. He knows it.

"I get the feeling you're avoiding me," Sally Clamp says as Bill tries to get past her office without her seeing him.

"No. Why would you say that?" Bill answers from the doorway to her office.

She slowly walks over to him. "You don't stop in to talk to me anymore, you run out of here when I'm not in the office, you don't kiss me anymore."

I never kissed you, he thinks. "Well, it wouldn't look good."

"Oh, but it would feel so good," she coos. Bill is getting sick. He turns to walk away. "Remember Bill, you'll always do well here, as long as I'm here. But I need to see something in return, and soon."

"Or?"

"Or nothing," Sally Clamp sweetly replies. Bill walks away, scratching his head. What did she mean by that? His chest now is getting tighter and tighter. God, how he would like to reach down his throat, and pull away the offending tissue that is clogging up his lungs, and putting such pressure on him. He'd love to do that, but he can't. Besides, it would be really messy.

Sarah walks by Bill's desk just as he reaches it. She seems to stop for an instant, but then she keeps on walking, without even acknowledging him. He hates her, he loves her, he hates her, he loves her. Bill just doesn't know. He doesn't know. Sarah knows. But she just won't tell him. And that angers and frustrates Bill the most. The women have the answers, but they refuse to tell the men. They let them flounder for a while, and allow them to try to figure it out on their own. But of course, they are not able to, because the women are not giving them the vital information needed to make a calm and rational decision. Bill hates the women, he loves them, he hates them. He doesn't know. He simply does not know. And it's really starting to get to him. It's all starting to build up inside him, looking for an outlet from which to explode. But the outlet is not there. Or rather, Bill is afraid to let it explode, fearing it will all come clear to him. And that is the most frightening thing of all.

-32-

Ah, the drive home Friday, Bill's favorite time of the week. Work is over, the weekend is here, not that Bill has been doing anything on the weekend except sitting at home and watching baseball, but it's the principle of the thing. The drive home on Friday is always so relaxing. But of course, it's just the calm before the storm. When he walks in, his damn mother in law is there, being her usual pain in the ass. "When isa Helen cominga back?" and that nonsense. Bill pulls up to the house, and sees behind his screen door is a closed front door. That means either she has the air conditioner on, which is doubtful, or she's not home. Bill unlocks the door, and indeed she's not home. There's no note or anything, but who cares, she's gone for a while. Bill goes upstairs to change. He sits on the edge of the bed, removes his tie, and takes off his shirt. Then he lowers his pants. But he stops when they get around his ankles. He begins looking at his crotch. He sees the outline of his penis. He rubs it through the underwear. Suddenly, it starts to stir. It begins to get hard, but it stops, because Bill stops. Except for those horrible dreams, he hasn't had an orgasm in months. He rubs it again, and it starts to get harder. He hasn't masterbated for years. He always wanted to masterbate with Helen, to watch her, as she watched him. But she never wanted to do it. Bill puts his hand under his underwear, and except for guiding his penis into Helen, he handles his erect penis for the first time since he can't remember when. He lowers his underwear and lies down on the bed, his unit standing at full attention. He rubs it up and down, like he did when he was a teenager. It feels good. Helen could never rub it like he could. But then he stops. He thinks about his mother in law and Helen and Sarah and Sally Clamp. He can't do this. He's a grown man. He only wants to have orgasms with women, when they give him one. He sits up, and begins to raise his underwear back up. But he stops. His penis is still throbbing. It wants so badly to come. So does Bill. But he doesn't want to. He does, but he doesn't. He doesn't know what to do. He sits there naked on his bed, his penis still erect, his breathing heavy. He did this hundreds of times growing up. What's so hard about it now? What's the big deal? He starts to rub again, but he stops. He starts. He stops. Then he thinks about his mother in law and Helen and Sarah and Sally Clamp again. The women. The women who are ruining his life. Fuck them, Bill thinks, fuck them. He starts to rub now, harder, faster. His heart is beating. His breathing is short. He rubs even faster. He can feel the oily pre ejaculatory fluid on his hand. And then he comes. It shoots out all over his hand and legs and chest. Just then, he hears the door unlock. Fuck, she's home! With semen dripping off him, Bill gathers up his shirt, and with his pants around his ankles, he runs as well as he can to the bathroom. "Heya Bill. What area you doing upa there?"

"Nothing," comes the meek cry from the bathroom, where Bill is sitting on the bowl.

"I heara you running?"

"I ran to the bathroom. I have diarrhea," Bill says as he wipes himself off with tissues, finding semen everywhere, as far up as his neck, as far down as his knees. Bill can't take a shower. She'd hear the water. But he can soap off, calling on his trusty bar of soap to clean up his dirty work. But when he reaches in the back of the cabinet, it's not there. He pushes everything out, and it's gone. The wrapper and all. Where could it be? He puts it back in the exact same spot every morning. Where could it-Her. She did it. Bill hurriedly puts on his shirt, picks up his pants, and runs downstairs.

"How'sa your diarrhea?"

"Enough about that," he says angrily. "Did you throw a bar of soap away from under the cabinet?"

"Yeah, I wasa cleaning."

"And you threw it away?!"

"Yeah."

"Why?!"

"Because it wasa disgusting. The wrapper was alla wet. And the soapa was almosta done anyway."

Now Bill is fuming. His soap is gone. "Did you ever think that soap belonged to somebody? That somebody other than you lives here? That you don't have free reign around here to throw things away as you please?"

"Hey, what'sa that smell? Smellsa like bleach."

Bill clenches his fist. His face is boiling. His heart is pounding. His breathing becomes short. His soap is gone. "Get out!"

"What?"

"Get out! Get all of your shit out of here, and get out. This is my home. You are not welcome here. You threw my soap away. Get out!"

"And where do you wanta me to go?"

"Go to hell for all I care, just get out!" Bill turns and walks upstairs. He lies down on his bed, listening to his mother in law whimper, and then leave. He begins to calm down. Suddenly, the pressure on his chest is gone. He can breathe freely again. He smiles. Suddenly, everything is clear to him. Fuck them, Bill thinks, fuck them indeed.

PART IV

-33-

The alarm clock goes off at its usual 6:00. Bill sits up and smiles. The also smiling newswoman tells Bill how these upcoming "dog days of August are not going to make you want to wag your tail." What does that mean, anyway? Well, it means one last heat wave is coming through, one more hot, sweltering weekend to get through before the Labor Day weekend comes around. Labor Day. The day Bill prays for every year. It means the summer is over. He survived unscathed. This year, Labor Day means more to him, since it'll mark the first time he makes love to Sarah. This past week, since he issued his edict to his mother in law, has been great. He wakes up in a good mood every day. He's happy, he's smiling, he's got a new bar of soap. Helen gave him hell. How dare he talk that way to her. She was all upset, she said. She couldn't stop crying, she said. She's still living with him, though. Helen says she needs time to find her a new place. But Bill doesn't care. He hasn't said a word to her since "The Incident" as he refers to it in his own mind. He never even looks at her. In fact, that is the way he's treating all of the women in his life. Helen calls to yell at him, but all he does is listen and hang up. Sally Clamp keeps asking him to talk, but he just walks right by. And Sarah, well, he'd ignore Sarah, too, but she seems to be beating him to the punch. This has been the happiest week of the summer. Bill hasn't said much of anything to anyone, except for his customers. And things are going quite well with them, thank you, without Sally's little tinkering of the numbers. He's back to his old self, promising things on which he knows he can't deliver, pressuring people, etc. Fuck those audio machines recording his every word. He'll do what he wants. He's Bill Press, the best seller at Prevail Marketing. And prevail he is doing, prevailing over everybody, by living by his rules, and forcing people to do the same. He feels as though he's accomplished something. He's taken back his life. Slowly and surely, he is regaining what the women took away from him: that all important stability he needs. When he wakes up now, he knows what to expect. His little life is nearly back into order. Yet his mother in law still lives with him. Helen still hasn't come back to him. Sally Clamp can fire him at any moment. And Sarah still doesn't give him the time of day.

He is still tormented by the laughter. He hears it more and more these days. It is clear. Something is laughing at him, as if his life is some sort of joke. He hears it whenever he thinks about Helen. He wonders if anyone else hears it. But no one does. He wonders if Helen hears it when she thinks about him. He wonders if she's as frightened of it as he is.

Will he ever get back with Helen? On one hand, he can't imagine life without her. When he thinks about having children and growing old, Helen is always there. But on the other hand, now that she's gone, he can see her never coming back. Once you go, sometimes there's no turning back. If only he had asked her to stay, things might be different now. If only he had asked her to come back just one time, maybe she would have. But now he's starting to sound like his mother in law. He's starting to sound like it's all over. But it's not. No decision has been made. He begins to hear it now. So he changes the subject, he thinks about the Mets fading down the stretch of the pennant race, and it mercifully goes away. How he wishes all of his problems would.

The newswoman was not kidding. It is hot. He flips on the radio in the car, to find out it's already 90 degrees, and it's expected to break the century mark later in the day, the first time all summer. That's a plateau not seen in these parts for a decade. But Bill insulates himself from this by rolling up his windows, turning on the air conditioning, and shutting out the outside world.

When he gets to work, he expects to hear Sally Clamp's voice calling after him, but her office door is shut. Maybe she's taking a three day weekend. He walks to his desk, looks over at Sarah's desk, but she's not there, either. Just as well, who needs the aggravation of not talking to these women. Today it's Bill's job to call women, and try to get them to take a free sample of disposable douches. His first call should be to his mother in law, but he's not talking to her. Anyway, it seems fewer and fewer women are douching these days, and the manufacturer wants to get women back into the habit. Bill tried to turn the assignment down, but Sally insisted, saying Bill is the man for the job, since he's the best.

"Hello?"

"Hello, is this Miss Natalie Gabriella?"

"Yes."

She sounds like she's maybe 21 years old. Bill gets a little nervous, but he must press on. "This is Bill Press. I'm calling you today from the Always Fresh company. Are you familiar with our products?"

"No."

"Oh." That makes things tougher. "Can I ask you a personal question?"

"It depends."

"Well, I'd just like to ask you how, well, how fresh you feel right now."

"What do you mean, fresh?"

"You know, fresh, clean."

"Well, I just took a shower, so I guess I'm clean."

She insists on making this hard. "Are you clean all over?"

"This is the weirdest conversation I've ever had."

"Tell me about it." After a long pause, Bill decides to change strategy. "Listen, how old are you?"

"20."

"Hmm. Do you have a boyfriend?"

"Yes."

"Are you close with him?"

"Yes."

"Very close?"

"Yes."

"When you're alone, what do you do."

"Is this the personal part?"

"Uh, yeah."

"Hey, is this some sort of sex quiz?"

Bill can see the audio machines rolling, just waiting for his answer. "Yes, yes it is."

"Cool."

"So, when you're alone, what do you do?"

"Well, we kiss."

"That's all?"

"No."

"What else do you do?"

"He bites my neck."

"And," Bill asks anxiously.

"And he likes to touch me."

"Where?"

"Oh, all over." Now she's teasing the overzealous questioner.

"Does he rub you breasts?" He can hear the whir of the machines.

"Yes."

"Does he lick your nipples."

"Yes."

Bill begins to get hard. "And then what does he do?"

"What do you think he does?" She's clearly enjoying this.

"Does he run his tongue down your stomach, all the way down, to your, your..."

"Cunt."

"Yeah."

"Is that what you like to do?"

"Yeah." Bill's heart is pounding. He's breathing faster. "Does he do that to you?"

"Yes."

"And then what?"

"And then he fucks me. He pounds the shit out of me, that's how hard he fucks me. But it feels so good. Is that what you want me to say?"

"Yeah." He's breathing harder now. And he's moving his hips around in his chair.

"And then I come. I feels so good. And then I take his dick in my mouth, and suck him off until he comes too. And then the come drips down my chin. And I stick my tongue out of my mouth, and lick it off. Do you like that?"

"Yeah."

"I'll bet you've got a hard on now, don't you?"

"Yeah."

"You'd like to come in my mouth, too, wouldn't you?"

"Yeah."

"Why don't you come now?"

"I can't. I'm at work."

"But you want to, don't you."

"Yeah."

"Then stick you hand under your desk, and rub yourself. No one can see." Bill does as he's told. He starts to rub himself through his pants. "Just pretend I'm sucking you off. I love your cock. Come in my mouth, come," she cries. And Bill does. The only detectable movement is a small jerk of his hips. "Did you come?"

"Yes."

"Good. Now you can tell me why you really called, you dirty old man."

"Well," a humiliated Bill begins, "I wanted to know if I could send you a free sample of the Always Fresh disposable douche."

"Douching. That's sick." And she hangs up. Immediately, all of the problems pertaining to what he just did hit him. Short term is the problem of semen seeping through his underwear and through his pants, where the whole world will see. He quickly runs to the men's room. Fortunately it's still early. And it's a Friday during the summer, so the entire staff is not in. No one saw him running. He goes into a stall, and removes his pants. There's a big stain on his underwear. He takes those off, too, and quickly realizes they can not be saved. He wipes himself clean, and puts on his pants, without underwear. The underwear he puts in the garbage can. During lunch, he'll go out and buy new underwear. He walks out of the bathroom, having just had an orgasm, and not wearing underwear, shaking his head, smiling almost. Damn women, they'll do it to you every time. And things were going so well, too.

-34-

"Listen Helen, it's time you made up your mind."

"About what?"

"You know about what."

"Yeah, I guess I do."

"It's been two months now. And I'm not going to wait forever. There are plenty of fish in the sea, so to speak, to keep waiting for you to decide what you're going to do."

"I know. You're right. But it's not easy."

"You've had two months. How much time do you need?"

"Well, I need more than two months. You can't consider throwing away six years of marriage in just two months."

"You know, I've been pretty patient with you. Going through your mood swings, all the uncertainty. But I'm telling you, I don't know how much more of this I can take. You have through next weekend. If you don't tell Bill you want a divorce, I'm throwing you out," Jerry says.

"That's very sympathetic. I thought we were friends."

"We're not friends. We're lovers."

"So, can't we be friends even if we decide not to be lovers?"

"No. You just can't turn it off like that. It's all or nothing."

"Apparently."

"You think you can be friends with Bill if you leave him for me?"

"I hope so."

"Forget it. He'll hate you, just like I'll hate you if you go back to him."

"That's nice."

"There's nothing nice about it. I'm going out." So now Helen will have to look for two apartments. One for her mother, and now one for her. Helen can always find a lovely little two bedroom, and live with her mother. No, that would be horrible. Imagine living alone with her. Look what it did to Bill. All she did was touch a bar of soap or something, and he went ballistic. Imagine what Helen would do if she touched her vibrator. Helen would probably kill her.

But maybe she won't have to find a place for herself. Maybe Bill will do a turnaround, and want her to come back. That'll never happen. He doesn't want it to. If he did, he never would have let her leave. Part of this was a test, to see if Bill would stop her from leaving. But when he didn't, she had to go through with it. When did it happen? When did he stop loving her? Helen hears the laughter now. It has grown to be a comfort, this laughter from unknown origins. It confirms her every theory. Helen wishes she could pinpoint the time Bill stopped loving her. Maybe it was something she did. Or was it something in Bill, something that made him draw away from her.

It's all so very sad. She used to be so happy. She remembers when they were first married. Bill used to get home from work before her sometimes. And there was always some kind of surprise. Sometimes he'd cook dinner for her. Sometimes he would hide, and wait for Helen to get undressed, then he would sneak up behind her, naked, his erect penis rubbing between her legs, his hands caressing her breasts. Other times when there was no surprise he'd just be sitting in the living room, watching television. And Helen would just stand there and watch him, thinking how lucky she is, that she has the perfect man. But maybe that never happened. Maybe it was just a movie she was watching. Because she really can't remember ever being happy. And that perhaps is the saddest thing of all.

Bill pulls up to his house. The Disagreeable Widow is standing by the door, waiting for him. "Bill," she screams out, the first words they have spoken in a week, "Helen's cominga over tonight."

"Oh yeah," he answers in a monotone.

"Yeah, aren'ta you excited."

"Yeah, sure," as he enters the house.

"You don'ta sound excited."

"Well, I am. This is me excited. Whooppee." He flips on the air conditioner.

"Anyway, she justa called."

"What did she say?" He begins closing the windows.

"She justa said she wantsa talka to you. Maybe she wantsa comea back."

"Maybe."

"Hey, whatsa wrong witha you?"

"What do you mean." He sits down on the couch.

"You're wife may be cominga back to you. And you don'ta care, do you?"

"Of course I care."

"No you don't."

Bill stands up, ready to yell. But why bother? She'll be gone soon. "Yes, I do." And he goes upstairs. He sits down on the edge of his bed. What if Helen really does want to come back? Why isn't Helen's little visit filling him with joy? Instead, he dreads it. He dreads what she has to say. Bill's not ready to get back with

Helen. He has to have sex with Sarah next weekend. If Helen's living with him, that will be difficult to do. But if Helen wants to come back, he can't say no. He has to let her. The conditioned air goes deep into Bill chest. The tightening begins instantly. It's more intense this time then it's ever been. The laughter is also louder. He tries to shut it off, by thinking of Helen's impending visit. But it only gets louder, his chest only gets tighter. It's in a vise, and this laughter is turning the screw.

Bill takes his pants off, and his flaccid penis falls out. He didn't get a chance to buy underwear on his lunch hour. In fact, it felt pretty good without underwear. He could rub his penis through his pocket whenever he wanted. Bill's been doing a lot of that in the past week, ever since that day his mother in law came home. It's like the floodgates opened. He realized he didn't need women to give him an orgasm. He could give himself one. So here he sits, alone with his dick. He thinks about today's episode at work, and he just doesn't feel like masterbating. It may feel good and all, but it's just not the same.

"Bill come ona down. Helen's here." Yeah, like he didn't hear the doorbell. And why did she ring the bell, anyway? It's her house, she could have walked right in. He says hi as he walks down the steps. He gets to the bottom, and is standing next to her. Helen waits for Bill to kiss her hello, but he doesn't. So she gives him a peck on the cheek. Big deal. Helen hugs and kisses her mother, and puts down her laundry bag. So that's why she came here. To do laundry. Good. She says she wants to put her laundry up, so she goes to the kitchen, where the small stackable washer-dryer is. "Why don'ta you go anda talka to her." Bill says he'll talk to her later. "Later, everything's later witha you." Shut up. Bill sits down on the couch. His mother in law sits next to him, on his right. Great. Helen comes over, and sits down on his left. He knew he should have sat on the chair. "So, what'sa new?" His mother in law nudges him in the ribs with her elbow. One of these days …Anyway, Helen says nothing is new, she's doing just fine, work is fine, her friend Jerry is fine, everything's fine. Helen and her mother are sitting too close to Bill. The air conditioning is on, but he starts to sweat. He can't even roll his shoulders without hitting into one of them. "Bill, tell Helen what'sa new witha you." Well, let's see, on the phone today at work, some hot little cunt made me jerk off until I came, and then I went the rest of the day without underwear. Instead, he says nothing is new, work is the same, life is just grand. Neither asks her mother what's new with her. No one really cares. The washing machine buzzes. "I'lla get it. You two talk." So she leaves. Finally, Bill has some breathing room. He moves away from Helen, but not all at once, lest she notice. He just inches away, little by little, so there's some room between them. And she never even knows. They make small talk. Bill avoids talking about Them, in fear she will tell him she wants to move back in. She doesn't talk about it either. They talk about the hot weather, about their cars, about nothing that matters. Helen's mother comes back, with a stupid grin on her face, like her leaving them alone will bring them back together. She takes her place next to Bill. She's sitting so close, he's got to move back towards Helen, giving up the territory he had just claimed. "So?," she says. So nothing, Helen and Bill say. "Oh." They sit there a while longer. Helen is just waiting for the dryer to buzz. Bill is growing increasingly more uncomfortable with these two women sitting so close to him. It seems as though they are sitting even closer to him. But that would be physically impossible. They are looking at him, as if they are waiting for him to say something. As if he knows what to do to make everything right. If anyone should say anything, it's Helen. She's the one who left. She's the one who doesn't know if she wants to stay married. She's the one who has to say if she wants to come back. But if she says it, Bill won't know what to do. Bill can hear the laughter again. He looks over to Helen. The look in her face tells him she can hear it too. Bill's chest is tightening, they are sitting too close to him, the laughter. Finally, he can't take it anymore. He jumps up. "What did you come here for?!" Even he doesn't know if he's talking to Helen, her mother, or the laughter. Helen speaks up, though. "I came here to do my laundry, and to see my mother." Oh. "And to see if you had anything to say." Yeah, I've got something to say. Next weekend, I'll be fucking an exciting woman. A woman who enjoys having sex. A wild woman who will let me do anything I want to do, and not go crazy if I stick some dildo up her twat. Okay? Instead, he says he ain't got nothin' to say.

-35-

Bill always kind of liked his dead father in law. And all through this separation thing, Bill has been thinking about him. He could be an ignorant Sicilian bastard sometimes, and he had a temper, especially when he was drinking, and that was every day. But he was a good man. Bill was sad when he died. He didn't cry, though. But he was sad nonetheless. Bill was the last one to see his dead body before they nailed the coffin shut and dropped him in the ground. It was the last moments of the wake, and everyone was gone except the immediate family. They all lined up to see him one last time. First, of course, Helen's mother, who looked at the body and ran out sobbing. Then Helen's brother took a quick look, and ran to console his mother. Then Helen looked, said some kind of Catholic prayer in Italian, and walked out. Last was Bill. This whole open coffin tradition was foreign to Bill. And in the two days of the wake, he refused to look the dead body in the face. But now, here he was, alone with the corpse. He looked at the face. He looked all right, for a dead person. Actually, he hadn't looked that well in months. He stood there, thinking about him. He had almost no sense of humor. But the things he did laugh at were the most bizarre. He'd laugh when he'd hear stories on the news about people dying violent and horrible deaths. He'd laugh at other people's misfortunes. To his credit, he laughed at his own as well. He'd probably laugh at Bill and Helen's crumbling marriage. Bill then patted the dead body on the arm, said goodbye, and walked out. Behind him, he could hear the funeral director walking in, and slamming the coffin shut forever.

Bill remembers the last conversation the three of them had. It was in the days before he died. He was ravaged by cancer. Helen and Bill would attempt to walk him around, just so he could get up from the bed. They were holding him up, dragging his feet really, when he stopped. He looked at both of them, and he said "You gotta makea me a promise." All right, sure. "Promisea me you two willa always be happy." Bill looked at Helen. They both smiled. Of course we will, Bill told him. He managed to muster a smile. They had made him happy in his dying days. But now, that promise is broken. Bill wonders if Helen remembers the conversation, wonders if it meant anything to her.

Breaking a promise to a dead man is about the worst thing you can do. When Helen wanted to get a cat, Bill, a noted cat hater, told a co-worker about his wife's whining. The guy told him not only would Bill get one cat, he'd have a few of them. Once you get a woman one cat, he told Bill, you can't stop her. You see, he explained, whether you hate cats or not, everyone has got to admit that kittens are the cutest things in the world. They look so dopey, with their big eyes and big ears and tiny faces. Well, once the kitten grows up and becomes a cat, they are not cute any longer. They are cats. Annoying, arrogant cats. So, he went on, the woman wants to relive the joys and pleasures of having a cute, adorable kitten around. So you give in, and buy her another one. Then another, then another. Women are so ridiculous. Once the thing grows up, they don't want it anymore. They always want to go back. They wish their cat could be a kitten again. But it's not possible. So they get a new one. What you've got to say to her, he said, is "Hey, you want a brand new kitten? Just wait until the cat dies, then you can get a new one. Now bring me a beer, woman!" They both laughed. And right there Bill vowed he would never, ever, get Helen a kitten. He didn't want to deal with a wife wishing their cat could become a kitten again. It was so ridiculous. A few months later, the guy died from throat cancer. He died a lonely man. He was never married. All he had, Bill found out later, was a 20 year old Persian, who ran out of the apartment when the paramedics who came to cart away his dead body left the door open. Outside for the first time ever, the cat didn't know what to do. So crossing its first street, it was flattened by a cab. The big street cleaner came by days later and sucked the Persian up into its huge vacuum.

-36-

"Hey Bill." Bill has failed for the first time in a week to slip by Sally Clamp's office. "How was your weekend?"

"Fine."

"Mine was great, thanks for asking."

"Did you miss me Friday?"

Friday, was she out Friday? "Yeah."

"Sarah wanted to have an extra day out there, so we went Thursday night."

"You and Sarah? Went where?"

"To her house in The Hamptons."

Bill is shocked. "You did?"

"Yeah, you should have come."

"I wasn't invited." But not to show her superiority over him, he adds "But I am going this coming weekend."

"Yes, I know."

"What'd you do out there?"

"Oh, lots of stuff. Went to the beach, went dancing, talked." Not about him, probably, knowing Sarah. Sally walks behind him, and closes the door. Still behind him, she wraps her arms around Bill, and starts rubbing his chest. "Oh, I've wanted to hold you all weekend. I've missed you so." The feeling of Sally's chubby body touching his disgusts him. She spins him around, and looks him in the eyes. Bill thinks Sally is going to kiss him, going to plunge that tongue down his throat. She opens her mouth, but thankfully, only words come out. "So, what about it?"

"What about what?"

"How many times are we going to have this conversation?"

"I don't know."

"Well I do. This is the last time. I've left you alone for a week, I never stopped you as you walked by my office. I was giving you time to decide. Well, time's up. I need to know what you're going to do."

Bill is scared. "Now?"

"Now would be nice." Now what does he say? "But you know what, I'm a nice girl. I don't want to pressure you or anything. So you don't have to tell me now. Soon, though, you'll have to tell me."

"When's soon?"

"Whenever I say it is." Oh. Bill turns to leave. He can't see Sally Clamp's beaming face behind him. "And don't forget," she continues, "it's my motivation that makes you the best seller at Prevail Marketing." Bill walks out. Soon. Soon could be tomorrow. It could be a week from now. It could be in five minutes. That's the problem with a word like soon. It's so indefinite. And what the hell was she doing at Sarah's house. Sarah said she wasn't going back out there until Labor Day. The lying bitch. There she is now. Bill decides to ignore her. He walks right by her, 'dissing' her, as the kids say.

"Hey Bill," comes the voice after him.

He turns around. "Hey Sarah." He hates her so much. "So, I guess this weekend is the weekend."

"What do you mean?"

"You know, this weekend, at your beach house?" I'll be fucking you?

"Oh, is that this weekend?"

"Yeah." She better not cancel, that bitch.

"Is it Labor Day already?"

At least she remembered what weekend was coming up. "Yeah, it is."

"Where does the summer go? It seems like just yesterday it was the first day of summer."

"Yeah, I know."

"So we leave Friday night, from here. You're driving."

"I know."

"Good." She saunters away. Bill sits at his desk and smiles. He thinks things are falling into place. He really does.

-37-

The last day in August is an important one is baseball. On September 1st, teams get to expand their rosters from 25 players, to 40. It's a time of big change in baseball. More than 400 new players now wear major league uniforms. On any given day in September, you can look at a boxscore, and not recognize half the guys. They are all young kids, being given a shot to show their stuff for a month in the majors. Except for the teams still in contention for a pennant. In those cases, the kids sit, while the veterans go for a divisional title.

It's a time when guys who got banged up during the year playing for a losing team take a break. It doesn't make any difference, since the team is going to lose anyway. Let the kids bust their butts while the old guys rest.

But sometimes the new kids make the veterans look bad. Sometimes it's hard to hit a new pitcher, even if the kid is 20 years old, and a veteran has been playing for 20 years. So often times, a kid will pitch a shutout his first time around. But the veterans are smart. After a few times up against the rookie, they figure him out. So if he pitches against the same team a couple of weeks later, they usually rack him around but good.

Bill hates this time of the baseball season. He likes having the consistency of a set lineup, of having 25 guys he knows on an almost intimate level. He knows how many homers they have, how many R.B.I.s, etc. But then the kids come up and disrupt everything. From one day to the next, Bill doesn't know who will be on the field: the veteran he's used to, or some new kid trying to make a name for himself.

In years past, this aggravated Bill to no end. If the Mets weren't in the hunt for the division, he'd just stop watching baseball entirely. Lately, though, he hasn't been so bothered by this. Sure, he'd still like to keep the rosters at 25 men, and keep the kids down on the farm until next year. But he's not so bothered that he stops watching games. He'll turn on a game, and not even watch who's playing. When you come right down to it, it doesn't really matter who's on the field. They still didn't win the pennant. Old or new, it's just another ballplayer.

-38-

Bill goes to the closet where they keep the suitcases. He opens it up, but instead of finding two large ones and one small one, there's only the one small one. He forgot Helen took the other two. Oh well, it'll have to do. He goes up to his bedroom, lays the bag on the bed, and unzips it. He walks over to his armoire, and opens up the underwear drawer. He takes out six pairs, and put them in the bag, Sure, he's only going to be gone three nights, but with all the sex he's going to be having, he's bound to soil at least a couple of pairs. And you can never have enough underwear. Then he goes to the sock drawer, and takes out six pairs of sweat socks, and three pairs of black dress socks. He places them in the bag. Next, he takes out six t-shirts, five bathing suits, and five pairs of shorts, and arranges them in the bag. It's nearly filled, and he hasn't even gone to the closet yet. From there he takes out four pairs of jeans, three pairs of dress slacks, and four button-down shirts. He piles them on top of what's already in the bag, and it's just too high. What can he spare? He takes out a t-shirt, but it makes no difference. Out goes a pair of jeans. He pushes down with all his might, and is able to get the bag closed. Now for the zippering. Bill proceeds to stuff the clothing that is trying to get out of the bag into the bag, as he attempts to zip around it.

Zipping and pushing, zipping and pushing, until finally it is shut. What he's left with is an extremely heavy, and an extremely odd shaped bag. It looks as if he's got bowling balls in there. Bill sits on it, to try to flatten it all out. But it doesn't work. But at least it's closed. Bill is not comfortable going away with only five t-shirts. He'll wear one Saturday, one Sunday, and one Monday. That will only leave him with two spares, just in case something happens. And that is not enough. But he dare not open the bag up, for fear of not closing it again.

Bill tosses the bag on the floor, making a loud thug. "What dida you do, falla down?" she asks from her bedroom, where she too is packing. Helen found her some apartment in some building somewhere. She's moving in this weekend. So when Bill comes back from his blissful weekend, she'll be gone, finally. Bill hopes he won't be coming back alone. He's hoping Sarah will not be able to get enough of him, so she'll want to come back home with him, and fuck him some more. Right on this bed. The idea of having sex with Sarah on the same bed he and Helen shared on their wedding night turns Bill on. It's as if the three of them are doing it together.

Although Bill always wanted to bring another woman home for him and Helen, he never wanted it to be Sarah. He wanted to keep Sarah all to himself. He didn't want Helen enjoying Sarah's wet pussy. That was something to be exclusively Bill's, not Helen's, not anybody's.

His mother in law barges in. "I'ma going toa sleep."

"Good night."

"I'lla be gone when you comea back."

"Yeah?"

"So I justa wanted to saya goodbye."

"Goodbye." She stood there for a moment. There are so many things she would like to say. Like why did he yell at her so much?

Like why did he look at her so oddly? Like why does he scream in the middle of the night? Like why doesn't he want Helen back? And that in some strange way, she actually enjoyed their time together. She really would like to say these things, to talk with Bill for a while. But she looks at him, watching him look at the floor, and she knows it's just not worth it. He'll learn some day, some day when he's a man. He's such a stupid fool. She can't believe he was ever married to her daughter. Neither could her dead husband. She can almost hear him laughing at the predicament the three of them are in. He's lucky he's dead, although if he wasn't, she wonders if any of this would have happened. Bill is still looking at the floor, as if he's afraid to look up. What a coward. Afraid to look at his own mother in law. What a cold, cold, boy. She leaves. Bill lets out a sigh of relief. And a tear, one single tear, rolls down his cheek.

-39-

Bill walks into work, beaming. Today is the day he's been waiting years for. He glides by Sally Clamp's office without as much as a peep from her. He guesses 'soon' has not yet arrived. And after this weekend, who'll care when soon is. He passes by his desk, and does a straight line for Sarah's. She's not there, but her travel bag is. It's much smaller, and much less lumpy than Bill's, but hey, she's probably got lots of clothes at the house already. Not that she'll have much need for clothing this weekend, heh, heh. Bill settles into his seat, and he sees a message at his desk. Helen called, call her back, she says it's important. There's only one important thing right now, and that's having sex with a woman named Sarah. He crumples up the note, and tosses it in the garbage can. What could be so important, anyway? That she wants to come back? Too late, baby, Bill's got plans this weekend. Maybe Tuesday, when his weekend of lust is over. And who knows if he'll want her back after making love to a real woman. Frigid, moody, crazy bitch. Who needs her?

Sally walks out of her office, and is heading for Bill's desk. Uh oh, here it comes. But she doesn't stop when she gets to Bill's desk. She doesn't even say hello. She just keeps on walking, until she gets to Sarah's desk. Sally leans over, to whisper something to her new pal. Sarah nods her head no, and they both giggle. Sally probably asked her if she has any spare tampons or some shit like that. Women. Sally heads back towards Bill, and gives him a sly smile as she walks by. Where has he seen that look before?

Sarah walks over. She looks behind Bill. "Where's your bag? You're not canceling, are you," she says in a slight panic. It's too late to buy a train ticket now.

"No, don't worry, I would never cancel on you. My bag's in the car."

"Oh good. So at 5:00, bring your car up front, then come in and call me from the lobby, and I'll come down."

"Okay."

"It's going to be a great time this weekend."

"I hope so," he says as he quickly raises and lowers his eyebrows.

"Yeah." Bill watches as she walks away. That tight little ass moving back and forth. In just a few short hours, he'll be digging his nails into that ass, as she rides him until he comes. "Whaddaya lookin' at?" Sally asks as she comes up on the other side of him.

"Uh, nothing."

"Okay. I just came over to say hello."

"Hello."

"See you later."

"Okay." Bill watches as she walks away. That big fat ass moving back and forth. It's amazing, they're both of the same gender.

As instructed, Bill walks over to Sarah at 5:00, and tells her he's bringing his car around. He'll call her when he's downstairs. He walks by Sally's office, and tells her to have a nice weekend. Oh, I will, she says. When he hits the street, the heat immediately hits him. It's hotter now than at noon. Those weathermen saying last weekend was the last blast of summer were wrong. As he walks the couple of blocks to the parking lot, he thinks about the weekend, how sex with Sarah is assured. Who would have thought even a few months ago that this was going to happen? That his wife would leave him, and he'd end up in bed with Sarah. The second part is a dream come true. But maybe dreams are not supposed to come true. Maybe dreams are supposed to stay as dreams, or they become nightmares.

Not very long ago, Bill was a happily married man. Now, he's running off for a weekend with another woman. Something seems so wrong about it. He should be running off with Helen for a romantic weekend somewhere, not with some selfish, vain bitch. A sexy selfish vain bitch. And that's what it all comes down to really, sex. Helen stopped having sex with him, and started having sex with that vibrator, and things turned sour. Or did things turn sour first? Bill doesn't know. But it doesn't really matter, does it?

Bill gets to his car and starts it up. It's here, it's really here. The weekend of a lifetime. But now that it's here, Bill doesn't know if he wants it. What he wants is to be with Helen. God, he wishes things with Helen were all right. But they're not. And he doesn't know what to do to make it right. He wishes he did. He pulls up in front of the building. Suddenly, there's a tremendous urge to put the car in drive, and just go home, and beg Helen to come back. His brain wants to do it. His foot wants to be on the brake, as his arm pulls the drive-shaft down three notches. But something else won't let him. His heart is pounding. He gets out of the car to call Sarah. It's too late.

Bill gets back in the car after calling Sarah. He presses a button, and pops the trunk open. He buries his face in his hands, with his elbows on the steering wheel. What have I done? What have I done? He hears a muffled "Hey Bill," coming from outside the closed, air conditioned car. He hears the trunk close. The passenger door opens. Sarah says hi and gets into the car. Bill's head slowly emerges from his hands. His eyes immediately focus on the rear view mirror, where he sees Sarah's smiling face. His hands still on his chin, he slowly turns to the right, where sitting in his passenger seat is a smirking Sally Clamp. "Bill," Sarah says from the back seat, still smiling, "Sally's coming along with us this weekend." Bill slowly turns away from Sally, and looks into the rear view mirror, to see Sarah's sly smile. Bill would love to smack that fucking smile off her face for good. Instead, he simply lowers his face back in his hands. What have I done? What have I done?

"This is my room," Sarah says as they walk down the hall. "You guys are staying in that room." She points down the hall. YOU guys! Bill has to sleep with Sally. Bill guesses soon has come and gone, and no one told him.

"You didn't way a word in the trip over here," Sally says to Bill as she begins to unpack. Bill still doesn't say anything. He just drops his lumpy bag on the floor, and sits on the bed, their bed. "Aren't you happy I'm here? This is a great way to get to know each other, you know, without the pressures of the office. Sarah really thought it would be a good idea."

"So," Bill speaks his first words in hours. It almost hurts his throat. "This was Sarah's idea."

"Yes. She came up with it while I was here last weekend. She said you would be coming this weekend, and she figured I should come to, you know, to keep you company."

Meaning Sarah keeps company with others. Now his blood is really boiling. All through the three hours of traffic in which they sat to get here, Bill was seething. And every time Sarah would laugh at something, that anger only increased. It's building up inside him, and there's no way to release it without insulting Sally, his boss, who holds the strings on his job. So with each little tid-bit of information he learns, the fire inside him gets that much hotter.

"Come on, we're going out," Sarah yells from the hallway. She walks into the room, and Bill's eyes pop out of his head. She's wearing a mini-dress. The bottom is just covering her ass, the top is just covering her breasts. "Let's go."

"I want to change first," says Bill.

"There's no time. We're already late."

"All right, let's go," Sally agrees. Bill begrudgingly complies, going out in the same clothes he put on at 7:00 in the morning.

"This is going to be fun," Sarah says as she adjusts her dress.

They go to some bar someplace that's wall to wall people. Sarah goes in first, and she immediately sees a guy she knows. She kisses him on the lips, and he puts his hands on her waist. The fire grows, the pressure builds. Bill just stands there with Sally. "Do you want a drink?" Sally shouts over the music.

"No," he answers. Sally gets one anyway, a gin and tonic. Bill looks over at Sarah, and she's surrounded by three guys. She's already got a bottle of beer in her hand. Bill watches as she lifts it to her mouth, puts it in, tilts her head back, and allows the liquid to go in. In a few hours, that bottle will be replaced with the dick of one of those guys. Bill's dick will be in Sally's mouth, probably. Somehow this weekend is not living up to its advance billing. Sally comes back, with her drink half gone already. "Sarah looks good," Sally shouts. Hmm. "I'm glad you're here. Last week, I stood at this crummy bar for hours while she flirted with every guy in here. I figured out of all the guys here, at least one would talk to me. But no one did." She waits for Bill to respond, but he doesn't. He's still looking at Sarah. "And then I had to listen as she had sex with them." This attracts Bill's attention.

"Them? How many did she have sex with?"

"I didn't mean 'them.' I meant have sex with one of those guys."

"Which guy?"

"I don't remember. What do you care, anyway?"

"I'm just curious."

"Why, do you want to ask him what it was like?"

"No."

"Yes you do. I know you want her. But face facts Bill, she doesn't want you."

Bill is stunned. "She said that?"

"No. But isn't it obvious? Isn't it obvious who wants you? I do, Bill. She's no good for you. She's a whore."

"Listen, let me set the record straight. I don't want anyone. I'm a married man."

"Oh really. Then why didn't the married man call his wife back today when she said it was important? I'm getting another drink." Bill resumes staring at Sarah. She finally looks over at Bill. They make eye contact. His anger goes away for a moment, to plead with her with his eyes: please, please stop all of this. But she just gives him that smile, takes a swig of beer, and puts her arms around a couple of guys. The anger returns, not to subside again.

Sally returns, though, with a drink in each hand. "Let's get drunk, Bill. Maybe it will loosen you up."

"I can't. I have to drive."

"Have just one."

"No. I'm going to the bathroom." Bill pushes and shoves his way to the men's room. He opens the door, and it hits a guy who's standing at the sink. "Sorry." The room is disgusting. There are paper towels all over the place, and it smells like piss. Bill doesn't even want to take his penis out in a place like this, but Sarah did not give him time to go to the bathroom after the trip out here.

"That girl is back again," the guy at the sink says to a guy in the stall.

"Yeah, I know. She looks hotter than ever in that dress." Can they be talking about Sarah?

"She brought her pig girlfriend with her again." They must be.

"But it's good. She ditches her, so you don't have to put up with the ugly one to get to the good looking one."

"Did you fuck her yet?"

"No, did you?"

"No, but from what I hear, half the regulars have. So I guess our turn is coming up." They both laugh. Then he asks Bill, "Hey, did you fuck her?"

"No, I didn't." The guy at the sink looks at Bill. It's clear Bill does not fit in with the conversation.

The guy in the stall adds, "Hey, if I don't get her, I'll go after the friend. I'll throw her a pity fuck." The guy in the stall laughs hysterically. The sink guy is still looking at Bill. "I'll meet you outside," he says to his buddy. Bill finishes his business, washes his hands thoroughly, and leaves. Still, though, he feels dirty.

"Gee, it was just like last week all over again," an already tipsy Sally says to Bill upon his return.

"Sorry," he shouts. The music seems louder. "I don't like this place."

"Me either," she states defiantly. "It's not our type of people. Let's get out of here. Let's ditch Sarah, and go back home and get to know each other a little better."

Bill thinks about it for a moment. "You know what? I'll have that drink now."

By the time 4:00AM rolls around, a drunk Sally is telling a dead-tired Bill the story of how when she was eight years old, she and a friend caught another girl cheating at jacks, so they threw the jacks at her, and one hit the girl in the left eye, and blinded her. Nice story. Sarah, meanwhile, is hanging all over some guy on the Dance floor that was created when the place began clearing out. When the song ends, the bartender shouts "Closing time." Finally, the night is ending. Sarah walks over with this guy, and announces he's coming home with them. Boil, boil, boil.

Sarah, the guy, and Sally make a bee-line down the hall. Sally breaks off, and goes into their bedroom, while Sarah and the guy continue into her's. They slam the door. Bill can still hear them giggling, though. Bill is left at the front of the hall. He's just standing there, wondering what to do. It's late, he's tired, he wants to go to bed. But Sally's in his bed. And she's got other things on her mind. Maybe she's got her period. Yeah, that would be good. Bill slowly walks down the hall, like a prisoner walking towards the electric chair. The prisoner has one up on Bill, though: a call from the governor can stop it, while there's no one that can stop Bill's executioner. Bill walks into the room, finding a smiling Sally lying on the bed, wearing only her bra and panties, the rolls of her belly hanging off of her, her fat thighs looking even larger spread out on the bed. Bill looks at the phone next to the bed. It's late, it won't ring. So Bill reaches for his toiletry bag, and heads across the hall to the bathroom. Once there, he washes his hands and face, and removes his contacts. Maybe Sally will find him unattractive in his glasses. Then he brushes his teeth, taking extra time to make sure he gets every single tooth. Maybe Sally will fall asleep if he takes too long in the bathroom. He can hear heavy breathing coming from Sarah's room. Bill then lowers his pants, and sits on the bowl. He doesn't have to go, he just doesn't know what else to do to kill time. After ten minutes of this, he decides enough is enough. Fate is calling him. It's out of his control. The gods made this happen, he might as well play it out, to see how it ends. As he walks from the bathroom to the bedroom, he can hear the bed squeaking from Sarah's room. The urge to burst in there and tell them to stop is so strong. He's making love to the woman Bill was supposed to be fucking. Now Bill starts to breathe harder, out of anger, and out of fear. He enters his room, and he smiles for the first time since the morning: Sally is asleep. He shuts the light, takes off his clothes, and crawls into bed. "Bill?"

Sally says in a drunken, tired voice. "Bill? I'm so sorry." Don't worry about it. "I didn't want it to be this way." I did. "She's not good enough for you." Sarah? "I love you." Yeah, yeah, yeah. "I just wanted you to love me." Go to sleep, fat girl. Sally falls soundly asleep. Bill tries to go to sleep, but he can hear Sarah and the guy going at it in the next room. He can hear the breathing and the squeaking and Sarah saying "Fuck me, fuck me." Bill begins to get an erection. He's never heard two people have sex before. Bill starts rubbing his dick. He would love to have some sex. He looks over at a sleeping Sally. He could easily slip her panties off, and fuck her silly. And she'd enjoy it, too. She wants it from him, she wants it bad. And so does Bill, only not from her. She deserves to get fucked that way, after she horned in on his and Sarah's weekend, how she's made his life a living hell these past few weeks, holding his job over his head like that. Everyone wants to screw their boss, now Bill can do it, literally and figuratively. With the sounds of Sarah and her guy in his ear, Bill rises from the bed, walks around to the foot of the bed, and starts to take Sally's underwear off. But as suddenly as he started, he stops. He looks at Sally's sleeping face. She doesn't deserve this. She's not an evil person, setting out to ruin Bill's life. All she wanted was some love. And love makes you do some strange things, things you normally wouldn't do. And who is he to punish Sally Clamp for wanting love? He crawls back under the covers, and resumes listening to Sarah. He hears more breathing, and the sounds of flesh slamming into flesh. Bill rubs his penis more. The breathing becomes louder now, and faster, and then it is quiet. Bill lays there, stroking his throbbing unit.

The silence from the other room is broken moments later, when he hears the guy ask "You want me to leave?" Bill doesn't hear the answer. "But how will I get home?" Bill thinks he hears something like I don't care. Bill hears the guy gather up his things, call Sarah a cunt, slam the bedroom door, and then slam the front door. Bill hears Sarah roll over, and then the house is silent again. She's even more of a bitch than Bill thought. Thank God he didn't have sex with her. She would have kicked him out, then he would have had to drive home in the dead of night. Bill is still nursing his hard-on. What were Sarah's intentions when she invited him out here? Was it to get Sally and Bill together? Probably not. She doesn't care about anyone else but herself. She just wants to get her way. She just wants to eat where she wants to eat. She just wants to get fucked, and then kick the guy out. Why did she invite him here? Bill continues to rub his dick. Did she just want him to see her in her hot little dress, and have him listen to her fuck some guy, just to say Look what you can't have? Bill begins to breathe even harder now. His anger is at a point at which it has never been. Why did she invite him here? He gets out of the bed, puts on his glasses, and goes into the hallway. He takes his underwear off, and opens the door to Sarah's bedroom. "I thought I told you to leave," she says angrily. Bill rips the cover off her of. She's lying there naked. Bill jumps on top of her, and bites her neck. "Bill?" He grabs her tits, and sucks on her nipples. "Bill!" Then he thrusts his rock hard penis into Sarah's still wet vagina. "Bill!" He pushes hard, and then pulls his dick out, and comes all over Sarah. They are both panting for breath now. She looks at him in the eyes. "I can't believe you did that." Bill runs out of the room and into his bedroom, quickly gets dressed, and runs out of the house to his car. Sarah still hasn't moved. "I can't believe he did that," she says out loud. She lifts her hand up, slowly brings it to her torso, and scoops up some of Bill's semen with her index finger.

She brings it to her mouth, and licks it off. Then she puts her hand back down, and pushes Bill's come towards her clitoris. She rubs herself with Bill's juices, until she comes.

-40-

It was dark, but she looked great naked. Her tits aren't big, and she was lying on her back, but they looked great. Her waist is so tight, not an ounce of fat on her. And her cunt was so wet. It was so hot, that's why he came so fast. It felt so good when he came. It had been building up inside him all day, along with the rage he was feeling. It was a violent outburst, as if the semen came screaming out of him, as if each drop that landed on her was saying Take that, bitch. She had it coming to her. All of those months of teasing him, especially these past couple of months. Inviting Sally Clamp to come out with them, and putting the two of them in the same bedroom, as if they were a couple, as if they had already slept together. And the way she kicked that guy out of her house after she was done with him. She just chews them up, and spits them out. But not Bill. Oh no, he had her on his terms, not her's. He fucked her, came on her, and left, left her lying there with his juices all over her. Now who's got the upper hand?

There's no traffic at 5:00 in the morning. It's great. You just sail on down the highway, doing 80. The windows are open, you can breathe like a normal human being. No buses on the side of you sending in noxious fumes to make you pass out. You're just free, there are no restraints. You can do whatever you want. You want to change lanes, you can change lanes. You want to slow down, you can slow down. You're in control. No one tells you what to do.

Of course, he'll be going to prison for what he did. Rape is against the law, whether she's a bitch or not, whether she was asking for it or not, whether she tormented you for months or not. When he gets home, he expects to have the police waiting for him. Maybe he'll stop and buy a gun, and go out in a blaze of glory like Dillinger. That bitch in the red dress. Or maybe he'll see the cops, turn around, and lead them on a cross country chase, that will end when he drives into the Grand Canyon. Nah, that's a chick thing to do. He'll take his punishment like a man, surrendering to the cops, pleading guilty, and going to prison. Maybe he'll meet a nice fellow behind bars who will make him his wife.

He's not going to prison. Sarah won't report anything. She wanted it. She wanted Bill to do what he did. She was asking for it, even begging for it. It was another of Sarah's little games: let's see how far I can push Bill, before he just takes me by force, the way I like to be taken. She never tried to fight him off. She wanted Bill's dick in her cunt. That's why she invited him out there.

This definitely is a pleasant ride. The sun is just beginning to rise in front of him. The bright orange sun peeking past the horizon, signaling the start of a new day. Bill feels good. He hasn't slept in nearly 24 hours, but he feels refreshed, almost reborn. He's tasted the forbidden fruit, and now it's time to start anew.

Suddenly, though, Bill slows down. Where is he racing to? He's got nowhere to go, no one to see. A wave of fear passes over him. Yes, the rising sun brings a new day, but what does that new day bring to Bill Press, the best seller at Prevail Marketing? Nothing. Bill hopes the police are waiting for him when he gets home. The idea of surrendering, of raising the white flag and finally admitting All right, I've had enough, is very appealing. His life used to be so simple, so orderly. He never had to worry about liking women, or women liking him. He was married. He didn't have to worry about such nonsense. Bill used to be so happy. He'd come home every day, Helen would be there, they'd eat dinner, they'd watch T.V., and go to sleep. It wasn't exciting, but it wasn't boring, either. It was life. At some point, though, it stopped being enough. Bill begins to hear the laughter now. He looks in the back seat, to see if someone's there, that's how clear it is. And in the back seat is the skeleton of his dead father in law, laughing hysterically. Bill wakes up when his car hits the dirt road of the shoulder. He's able to slam on the brakes, and steer the car straight, until he finally stops. But the laughter doesn't stop. He looks in the back seat to confirm that the earlier presence was just a dream. It was, but still the laughter persists. He takes a deep breath, and resumes his journey home. He's going a little slower this time, his eyes are open a little wider, moving every now and then to his rear view mirror, to check on the back seat.

Bill finally arrives home. His neighbors are piling the kids into their cars, to begin their weekend of fun. They all look at Bill as he walks by. It's apparent to them by his disheveled look that his weekend of fun has come and gone. No cops. That's good. Bill enters his house. He expects to hear somebody, something. But all is quiet. The air conditioner is off, Helen is not there, her mother is not there. She left after he did on Friday, never to return. He looks around for a note from her, saying goodbye, maybe thanking him for allowing her to live in his home, but there is none. A note would have been nice. So would some food. But she didn't leave any of the leftovers. She took them all with her. Bill hasn't eaten since his lunch break from work Friday. He hoped to have eaten once they got out to the beach Friday night, but that never happened. He mulls around the house a bit, nothing to eat, nothing to do. He should go to sleep, but he doesn't want to. He's afraid if he goes to sleep, and there's no one here to wake him up, he'd sleep forever, and probably no one would miss him. That's what happened to that guy at work. It took a couple of days before people realized he was missing. The poor cat. She must have jumped on him, bit his nose, licked his face, without even knowing he was dead. And then the way the cat was left dead in the street. You can only take care of yourself up to a point. But when you really need someone, no one is there for you. The exhaustion is getting to Bill. He trudges upstairs, and falls into bed, without taking his clothes off, without eating, without anything. There's no one there to help him. He's alone.

The phone wakes him up. Who can it be? Helen? Telling him she wants to come back? Sarah? Accusing him of rape? Sally? Telling him it's all right if he doesn't love her? "Hello?"

"Bill? You sound horrible."

"Thanks, Helen."

"What are you doing there?"

"I live here, remember?"

"Don't get snotty. It's just that mom told me she saw you packing."

"So if you didn't think I'd be here, why'd you call?" Bill hates that.

"I was just going to leave you a message. We need to talk."

"Okay, talk."

"Not over the phone."

"Okay. Why don't you come over tomorrow?"

"I can't."

"Why?"

"Moving."

"Oh, helping your mother get settled?"

She doesn't answer. "How about Monday?"

"Fine."

"Maybe we'll have a little barbecue, for old times sake."

"Yeah, okay."

"So why were you packing? Are you leaving too?" Helen chuckles, but Bill is not in the mood.

"No. I was packing for the weekend."

"Where are you going?"

"Hamptons."

"When are you going?"

"Already gone, and now I'm back."

"Short weekend."

"Yeah, I'll see you Monday, like noon or something." He hangs up. He gets out of bed, his clothes sticking to his sweaty body. He never did turn the air conditioner back on. He smells. He smells like beer and smoke and sex and body odor. He walks to the bathroom, and strips off all of his clothes. He dumps them in the hamper. He looks in the mirror. He needs a shave. He turns on the shower, but before stepping in, he reaches into the back of the vanity, and takes out Bar of Soap Number Two. He steps into the shower with it. It's almost brand new, just a couple of weeks old. It's still pure white. He can still see the name on it. He looks at it. Then he reaches his hand back through the shower curtain, and throws it in the garbage. He reaches for the soap already in the shower, and proceeds to cleanse himself.

Bill settles in front of the television with his peanut butter and jelly sandwich and a glass of Pepsi. It's late in the afternoon, and the Mets game is nearly over. It's in the eighth inning, the Mets are losing 7-3, and no one Bill has ever heard of is on the field. It looks like the Mets are content to just go through the motions for the rest of the season, not even caring about the outcome. If Bill was the manager, he would do just the opposite. He would make the decision to win. Why bother playing the game, if you're not going to do everything it takes to have a good outcome?

Saturday night. Bill has spent every Saturday night at home
since Helen left. But he was never alone, because her mother was
there. He begins to think about his teenaged years, before he met
Helen. He spent many a Saturday night at home. Sometimes his
parents were home, sometimes his brother was there. But other
times, he was alone. He'd watch "The Love Boat" and "Fantasy
Island" and go into his father's underwear drawer and read his
stash of Playboy magazines. As he played with himself, he'd think
about some of his friends who were probably out with real girls,
thinking someday, he won't have to be alone on Saturday night
anymore. That was one of the best things when he started dating
Helen. She was always there for him Saturday night. He didn't
have to bring himself to orgasm anymore. He had a girl to do it
for him. And now a decade later, here is Bill on a Saturday night,
aroused by his memories, playing with himself. He stops, though,
pulls up his pants, puts on his shoes, and heads out the door.

He pulls up to the bar. It's much more crowded tonight than the
night he saw Stacy Wellman there. Unlike the bar in The
Hamptons last night, this place is filled with older people. It's a
neighborhood bar, not a pickup joint. People come here to be with
people they know. Bill finds room at the bar, and sees the ashtray
where he left his wedding ring. He fishes around in it, but of
course it's not there. He orders a beer. He looks down the bar.
Everyone sitting there looks sad. They all have drinks in front of
them, their chins resting on their hands. It looks like they are all
there to forget their problems. But it's impossible to do, because
all they have to do is turn around and look at the next person, and
they are reminded of why they are there. Bill slowly sips his beer,
still repulsed by the taste of it. But at least he's not home by himself. He's here, in the company of others, in the company of other
lonely people. He should find a certain comfort in this, but he

does not. He still feels like he did in that Chinese restaurant. He still thinks everyone is looking at him, although there are dozens of Bill Presses in this place, sitting alone, sipping a drink. He now feels sorry for Sally Clamp, the way Sarah abandoned her in that bar last week, leaving the poor little fat girl sitting there by herself, not knowing guys are talking about her in the bathroom. Poor, poor Sally Clamp. Unrequited love is the worst kind. You sit there and pine away for a person, only to have them spit in your face. No one deserves that. Bill doesn't feel guilty, though. He's not the one who made Sally love him. He never approached her. It's all in her mind. It has nothing to do with him. Bill's so happy he's never been the victim of unrequited love. Sarah doesn't count, because he never really loved her. He just wanted to have sexual intercourse with her. And Helen, well, it's not his fault. Bill looks in the mirror behind the bar. He sees the beer bottle sitting in front of him, his chin resting on his hand. He looks like all the rest of the poor saps at the bar. There are dozens of them. Why would anyone be looking at him?

-41-

Bill looks in the mirror. He needs a shave. He's been saying that for three days now. Helen is coming today. He should probably shave. He shrugs his shoulders and walks out of the bathroom. Every day for the past few years, the house was filled with people on Labor Day, people lamenting the end of summer. But before you knew it, another summer was upon you, and soon another Labor Day. The years pass so quickly now. When Bill was a kid, it seemed like school would never end, and summer would never come. And then the summer seemed to last forever. Time stood still. But when you grow up, time just seems to slip away. And before you know it, years have passed, and you haven't done a thing. The doorbell rings. Helen's here. They exchange pleasantries. They sit down on the couch. "So, what do you want to talk about?" Bill asks.

"Let's not talk right away. Let's barbecue first."

"Barbecue?"

"Yes, remember I said maybe we can barbecue for old times sake, and you said 'fine?'"

"Oh yeah. I forgot." Helen's eyes fill up with tears, and they start to roll down her cheek. "Why are you crying?"

"I just wanted to have a nice day with you," she sobs, "like it used to be."

"Things aren't like they used to be, Helen."

"Oh, you've finally realized it?"

"Yes."

"Took you long enough."

"Well, it's a hard thing to admit, don't you think?"

"Yes."

"We used to be so happy. Remember? We just used to sit here on the couch, and watch T.V., and laugh. We really were happy, weren't we?" Now it's Bill's eyes filling up with tears.

Helen cries more. "Yes, we were."

"Well, then why can't I remember?" a teary Bill asks.

"I don't know. Probably the same reason I can't."

"That's really sad, isn't it?"

"Yes." They sit there for a minute, looking at each other, crying. Then they embrace, and they both hear the laughter. It begins to fade away, never to be heard from again. The torment is over. It's just like finally figuring out a recurring dream. Once you know what it's all about, you never have it again.

-42-

Fall is in the air. Bill can smell it. His lungs are clear, he can breathe freely, without the fear of artificially conditioned air clogging up his breathing passages. He feels good. The four day growth on his face gives Bill that rugged look he loves so much. He doesn't have to shave anymore. He's got no one to impress. He walks past Sally Clamp's office. "Bill, may I see you a moment." He walks in, expecting to see Sally on her knees, asking for his forgiveness. Instead, she's sitting behind her desk. A man is sitting on a chair in front of the desk. Bill doesn't recognize the back of his head. "You know Mr. Prevail."

"Good morning, sir." He doesn't say anything.

"Sit down, Bill." Bill sits in the chair next to Mr. Prevail. "This is a very difficult thing to talk about. On Friday, one of the supervisors was spot-checking the tapes. You are aware Bill we tape all of the phone calls here."

"Yes, I am."

"And one tape the supervisor listened to was quite disturbing. He gave it to Mr. Prevail, and he gave it to me. You were talking to a young woman, and you told her you were conducting a sex survey. And-"

Bill interrupts her. "Yes, I know what you're talking about."

"Good," Mr. Prevail finally speaks up. "Then you know you're fired. You're a very sick man, Mr. Press. Saying you're conducting a sex survey, and then asking her about her sexual habits, and then asking her for a date. We can't have that type of thing going on at Prevail Marketing. Clean out your desk. I want you out of here immediately." He walks out of the office. Bill looks at Sally.

"How long have you had that tape?"

"What do you mean?"

"You know what I mean. Prevail never heard that tape, because I never asked that girl out on a date. I just...well, you know what I did. How long have you been personally monitoring my phone calls?"

"Listen, I didn't want to do this. All I wanted to do was love you. And what do you do? You make love with Sarah while I slept in the next room."

"She told you?"

"Yes, she told me everything."

"Oh. Was she, like, mad?"

"Of course, she's so damn selfish, of course something like that would make her angry. But I don't want to talk about that, and I don't want to talk to you. Just get out of here." Bill gets up to leave. He'd like to say he's sorry, but the words just don't come out. He can hear Sally sniffling as he walks out of the office. As he walks towards his desk, his former desk, actually, he runs into Sarah. She looks at him, with fire in her eyes. He opens his mouth to say he's sorry, but a furious Sarah cuts him off.

"Don't even say it. How dare you? How dare you do that to me? How dare you come before I come?"

"What?"

"Listen, I don't care if you've got some kind of premature ejaculation problem or what, but I always come first, got it?" She turns and walks away. Bill can only shake his head. He goes to his desk, and begins cleaning out the drawers. The phone rings. He lets it ring once, then twice, and decides to answer it, just one last time.

"Prevail Marketing."

"Bill Press please."

"Speaking."

"Hello, this is Mrs. Harrington. You sold me a subscription to the Daily News earlier this summer. And you said if I didn't like it, to call you back the day after Labor Day, and you'd give me my money back?"

"Yes."

"Well, I didn't like the way things went this summer, and I want things to go back to the way they were before." Bill smiles. Ah, if it were only that easy.

Printed in the United States
3945